There was something about Turner McLeod...

Lacy stewed for several minutes, thinking up terrible things to say to the man who changed personalities so fast, she never knew what to expect. He'd been friendly and kind—and then angry and threatening.

She found herself once again thinking about the sequence of events that had led to their kiss.

She'd been innocent of ulterior motives. She'd gone to wake him from a nightmare. And then he'd grabbed her and kissed her and...she'd kissed him back. That was the part that made her squirm with embarrassment. She could have stopped the kiss. But she'd given herself to it with unexpected, heated passion.

She didn't know Turner. Had no reason to trust him. He'd been labeled a fire starter—and she'd been kissing him like some schoolgirl with a bad crush.

What was wrong with her? Why had she kissed Turner McLeod back?

Dear Harlequin Intrigue Reader,

We have another great selection of exciting Harlequin Intrigue titles for you this month, kicking off with the second book in Rebecca York's 43 LIGHT STREET trilogy MINE TO KEEP. *Never Alone* is a very special story about the power of love and the lengths to which a man and woman will go to find each other—no matter the obstacles.

One down—three to go! Our MONTANA CONFIDENTIAL series continues with *Special Assignment: Baby* by Debra Webb. A covert operation and a cuddly baby are just a day's work for this sexy cowboy agent. And Caroline Burnes scorches the sheets in *Midnight Burning*, a story about one man's curse and his quest for redemption.

Finally, come play HIDE AND SEEK with Susan Kearney as she launches her new three-book miniseries with *The Hidden Years*.

So pick up all four for a dynamic reading experience.

Sincerely,

Denise O'Sullivan
Associate Senior Editor
Harlequin Intrigue

P.S. Next month Harlequin Intrigue proudly welcomes back Anne Stuart and Gayle Wilson in *Night and Day*, an extraordinary 2-in-1 keeper!

MIDNIGHT BURNING

CAROLINE BURNES

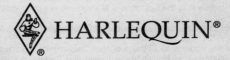

HARLEQUIN®

TORONTO • NEW YORK • LONDON
AMSTERDAM • PARIS • SYDNEY • HAMBURG
STOCKHOLM • ATHENS • TOKYO • MILAN • MADRID
PRAGUE • WARSAW • BUDAPEST • AUCKLAND

ISBN 0-373-22635-7

MIDNIGHT BURNING

ABOUT THE AUTHOR

Caroline Burnes continues her life as doorman and can opener for her six cats and three dogs. E. A. Poe, the prototype cat for Familiar, rules as king of the ranch, followed by his lieutenants, Miss Vesta, Gumbo, Chester, Maggie the Cat and Ash. The dogs, though a more lowly life form, are tolerated as foot soldiers by the cats. They are Sweetie Pie, Maybelline and Corky.

Books by Caroline Burnes

HARLEQUIN INTRIGUE

86—A DEADLY BREED
100—MEASURE OF DECEIT
115—PHANTOM FILLY
134—FEAR FAMILIAR*
154—THE JAGUAR'S EYE
186—DEADLY CURRENTS
204—FATAL INGREDIENTS
215—TOO FAMILIAR*
229—HOODWINKED
241—FLESH AND BLOOD
256—THRICE FAMILIAR*
267—CUTTING EDGE
277—SHADES OF FAMILIAR*
293—FAMILIAR REMEDY*
322—FAMILIAR TALE*
343—BEWITCHING FAMILIAR*
399—A CHRISTMAS KISS
409—MIDNIGHT PREY
426—FAMILIAR HEART*
452—FAMILIAR FIRE*
485—REMEMBER ME, COWBOY
502—FAMILIAR VALENTINE*

525—AFTER DARK
       "Familiar Stranger"*
542—FAMILIAR CHRISTMAS*
554—TEXAS MIDNIGHT
570—FAMILIAR OBSESSION*
614—FAMILIAR LULLABY*
635—MIDNIGHT BURNING

*Fear Familiar

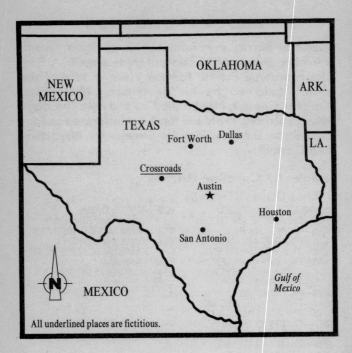

All underlined places are fictitious.

CAST OF CHARACTERS

Lacy Wade—Lacy isn't where she wants to be as a journalist, but she finally has her chance to publish an article in *Texas Legends* magazine and begin the career she's worked so hard to attain. She'll do anything to convince Turner McLeod to talk.

Turner McLeod—Misfortune and ugly rumors have followed him since he was a teenager. A solitary man, Turner has steadfastly refused to defend himself against the gossip and accusations...until he meets Lacy.

Melton Weeks—Owner and operator of Weeks Supply, a small grocery on the edge of the Texas wilds, Melvin is a local character. When his small store burns under strange circumstances, Lacy must determine if Melvin is a victim or part of the plot.

Anthony Ascenti—When his sister died in a mysterious fire, Anthony lost a big part of his life. Since that moment he's been set on revenge, and the man he holds responsible for Lilith's death is Turner McLeod.

Lonnie Larue—A friend of the family, Lonnie is loyal to a fault. He's with Anthony 100 percent in all of his plans. But what role does Lonnie play in Anthony's past?

Erin Brown—Editor of *Texas Legends* magazine, Erin wants a story more than anything else, but is there an ulterior motive behind her determination to find out the truth about Turner McLeod?

To all my Texas friends.
May they never settle down.

Chapter One

The night-light beside the huge oak cast strange and twisted shadows on the ground. Turner moved slowly through them, stepping on the tangled pattern of limbs etched in the lawn. His boots seemed to whisper through the dew-soaked grass, and the night was filled with the magic of nature.

At the edge of the light he slowed and looked at the small house that was his destination. The Creole cottage held everything he'd ever dreamed of having, and in the wonder of the night it was touched with fairy magic. Behind him the Bayou Teche slipped quietly, lazily by toward the Gulf of Mexico.

All around him St. Martinsville was silent, a beautiful sleepy little town lulled into rest. He thought of Lilith, the woman who slept in the small cottage by the Teche, the place he'd come to view as home. She was the rose that bloomed only for him.

He lingered in the darkness, enjoying the smell of the river and the quiet of a resting town. A breeze sprang up, fluttering the oak tree behind him and ruffling the curtains in her window. He could see her, the sheet pulled up to her waist and the thin cotton nightgown with the lace at the throat. She loved sleep-

*ing with the windows open so that the night smells
and sounds were all around her. She'd grown up in
a small town where there was nothing to be feared.
Where an open window wasn't an invitation to disaster, no matter how many times he'd tried to warn her.
His own thought made him shift uncomfortably. But
Lilith had banished those things from his life.*

*In the darkness he smiled. It was her innocence that
had begun to heal him. Perhaps there was a place
where evil wouldn't follow him. Lilith was the charm,
the gris-gris—a word he'd learned from her—that
warded off the evil eye.*

*His anticipation at seeing her, touching her, stirred
him into motion. He'd lingered long enough in the
shadows. Though she was asleep, she was waiting for
him. She'd left the door unlocked for his return.*

*Above him the tree fluttered encouragement, and he
started toward the door.*

*At first he thought the acrid scent was his imagi-
nation. He stopped and sniffed. The light breeze
shifted erratically and he let out a sigh. It was just
the past trying to creep in and steal his happiness.
There was no fire.*

*The white lace curtains in Lilith's window danced
an invitation, and he started forward again, this time
without hesitation. His anticipation was so great he
wanted to run to her. He wanted to kiss her eyelids
so that her dark eyes would open with desire and he
could melt into them. Yes, Lilith knew a few things
about magic, especially about charms. She had captured him completely, and he was the most willing of
prisoners.*

*He focused on her window, and when he saw the
slow and lazy form moving from the roof of the cot-*

tage, he had to slow down to examine it more closely. It was ghostly, wavering in the night sky.

The smell of the fire struck him suddenly and with great force just as the orange flames burst through the roof, hungrily trying to gobble the night sky.

With the horrible smell came a tidal wave of nausea and the sense of physical restraint. Turner didn't understand where the ropes came from, but suddenly he was bound. He felt the bark of the oak tree biting into his hands as he pressed against it, trying to free himself.

Even as he struggled against the bonds, the orange flames licked the sky, then turned back to devour the roof of Lilith's cottage. The lace curtains burst into flame, and Turner began to shout her name, but no sound came from his throat. No matter how furiously he tried to yell, to wake Lilith, the only sound he made was a groan.

Tied to the tree, he could only watch as the fire grew hotter and hotter, eating through the house until the roof collapsed. He had to get free—he had to save her. He threw himself against the restraints that held him and a hoarse cry burst from his throat.

TURNER MCLEOD sat up in bed, the sheets so tangled around his chest and legs that he could barely move. His heart felt as if a train had struck his chest, and he realized his face was wet with sweat, and possibly tears. He began to shiver as the familiar chill of an aftershock swept over him. With a low moan he fell back against his battered pillow.

A cold wet nose pressed into his side and he reached over to give the German shepherd a pat. It was the dream. The same dream he'd had again and

again. That he'd dreamed it exactly the same way at
least a hundred times took none of its power away—
it still gripped him with such emotional force that he
often thought death would be preferable.

And then the agony would begin to abate. Reality
would march to the rescue, and he would recite the
litany of facts that he used to ward off his guilt. He
had not been in St. Martinsville, Louisiana, when Lilith's house caught fire and burned. He had been hours
away, headed for Texas. Lilith would not have been
lying in bed, waiting for him. She had, in fact, broken
off their relationship. She'd given him no explanation,
no reason or word of comfort. She'd merely told him
that she didn't want to see him again, and then she'd
closed her door and locked it—something he'd never
heard her do before.

That she'd died by fire was a fact he couldn't
change. Fire. An elemental force, a powerful force of
life or destruction. In his life he'd met only the de-
structive side of it.

Fire starter. It was an ugly term, one that implied
the worst of human nature, a person who deliberately
burned homes and businesses and woods and barns
for profit or revenge. Fire starter. How often had he
heard it?

"Watch out for Turner McLeod. Wherever he goes,
flames follow." That whisper had marked his life for
the past fifteen years.

Yes, he'd heard them more than once. Five times,
to be exact. Five tragic fires that seemed to combust
if he happened to walk by a particular building on a
particular day.

There was no scientifically satisfactory explanation
for it. Probably never would be. Turner had only to

live with the consequences and the coincidences. The hard facts were that in the past eighteen years there had been five major fires involving the property of someone who had wronged him in some way. And in the last fire, Lilith had died. Was it because he subconsciously wanted to punish her for breaking up with him? Was there some power there, deep within his brain, that answered his summons for revenge?

The answer was no. Lilith had turned away from him, but he'd never wanted to punish her. Never. He'd been stunned and hurt by her rejection, but he'd packed his things and left. Never in his wildest fantasies had he wished the smallest injury to her. He'd had nothing to do with the fire.

He abruptly got out of bed. Rex, whining softly, followed him over to the stove. The rustic cabin was only one room, with the wood-burning stove, a big bed covered with at least a half-dozen quilts, and a couple of chairs and a table. It wasn't home, because Turner didn't have a home. Didn't want one. His home was the road, and though he didn't believe he was a fire starter, he did know he had one true talent—leaving. He was damn good at that.

He put the water on for coffee and sat down in one of the chairs. Outside it was still dark, at least an hour before sunrise. An hour until he could start his quest once again. After the dream there was only one thing that kept him going, and that was his search.

LACY WADE SAT perfectly erect in the big wing chair. She held her breath, determined not to tug at the brand-new, expensive—and uncomfortable—suit as she watched Erin Brown pick up a contract, read a moment, lower it and then look up at Lacy.

"I normally don't like to send new employees out into the field," Erin said slowly, her green eyes narrowing as she thought. "But we need this story and we need it now. If I hire you on a preliminary short-term contract, there's no one else to do it but you." She tapped her half-inch-long red nails against a gold pen and studied Lacy.

"I can do it." Lacy didn't know what the story was, but she didn't have a choice. She needed a job, and whatever it took, she was going to do it.

Erin grinned. "You have spunk. That's very important for a writer for *Texas Legends*. Spunk will open a lot of doors."

"I can get this story," Lacy said, understanding that now was the time to show self-confidence. "I can get it and I can write it."

Erin's smile widened. "I like your style, Lacy. You're inexperienced, but everyone has to have a start. I wish I could team you with one of our older writers—give you a chance to work with someone who knows the ropes. Unfortunately I want someone on this Turner McLeod guy for the January issue. That means a two-week turnaround. That doesn't give me any waiting room. If I hire you, you'll leave right away for the hill country."

"I can do that."

"Could be some camping involved." Erin's eyebrows were arched in question.

Lacy hated camping. *Hated* it. "I can do that, too."

"I want updates every day."

"Cell phone," she said. "Shouldn't be a problem."

"And you have to convince this man to talk to you, to tell you about himself. He has to learn to trust you.'' She leaned forward. ''And he has to tell you his innermost secrets.''

Lacy wished she could stand up and simply walk out. This wasn't the job she wanted. But it was the job she had to have. If she was ever going to become a writer, she had to start someplace. *Texas Legends* was the only magazine that had responded to her résumé. Out of a hundred letters sent, this was the only reply she'd gotten. If she couldn't land a writing job, she'd have to go back to the hair salon where she'd worked the past ten years. Her college degree in writing—earned at great sacrifice at night—would be worthless.

''I spent the last ten years listening to secrets,'' Lacy said. ''It's been my experience that if a person has a sympathetic audience, he or she will tell a lot of personal details.'' Of course, listening to her hair clients with a sympathetic ear was a lot different from soliciting secrets to print in a magazine that had the reputation of being little better than the worst tabloid.

''Turner McLeod is going to be hard to flip,'' Erin said. She pushed her chair back from the desk and began to swing her crossed leg as she thought. ''He's on some kind of quest. You know, the purple wildebeest that cures rickets or something of that sort. He's always chasing down myths and legends, but I think mostly it's an excuse to be alone in the woods. I guess if I had to pick a word to describe him, it would be loner.'' She stopped swinging her leg. ''Unless the other word is more accurate.''

''The other word?'' Lacy asked.

''Folks say he's a fire starter.'' Erin's teeth gleamed. ''They say wherever he goes, fire follows.''

''He deliberately sets things on fire?'' Lacy felt the

chill fingers of disquiet crawl up her spine. She did her best not to show it. "Why?"

Erin's eyebrows lifted and her satisfaction with Lacy's reaction was obvious. "There are two theories. The most logical one is that he gets angry at someone and then sets the fire in an act of revenge."

Lacy felt her gut twist. This wasn't exactly someone she wanted to be alone with in the wilderness. What if he found out she was bird-dogging him to write him up in a magazine? That might not make him very happy.

"The other theory is that he can't help starting the fires. Sort of a spontaneous-combustion thing. You know, he gets angry or whatever and the fires just happen."

To Lacy that sounded even more dangerous than revenge fires. The man could get angry and fireballs would start hurtling at her.

"You look skeptical, dear," Erin said with a nasty undertone.

"Not skeptical, just weighing the data." Lacy didn't want this job. But in her life, opportunity wasn't something to walk away from. She'd raised her brother and sister and given them the college education she'd denied herself until last. Here she was being offered a paying job to write. She would take it, and she would show Erin Brown what she could do.

"This sounds perfect," Lacy said. "Turner McLeod, myth hunter and fire starter. I think it belongs on the cover." If she was going to do this, she was going to reap the benefits of her efforts.

"You get the scoop on this man and I promise you

the cover,'' Erin said, standing up as she handed the contract across the desk for Lacy to sign.

"This is a single-story contract with a payment schedule. I'll give you five thousand on signing and the remaining fifteen when you complete the story. If you bring this in on deadline, you'll be offered a full-time staff position. It's all here in black and white.''

Lacy took the contract with trembling hands. Twenty thousand dollars for one story! It was incredible.

Erin reached into a drawer and took out a checkbook. She hastily scribbled across a check, tore it out and handed it to Lacy. ''Here's five thousand for expenses. I hear McLeod's way up in the wilderness. You'll need camping gear and a horse.''

"A horse?'' Lacy hadn't bargained on this.

"Unless you really like packing a lot of gear on your back up steep trails. I hear McLeod has a horse and a dog.''

"Okay.'' Lacy knew where to buy camping gear, but how did one go about securing a horse?

"I'll get my secretary to find a rental agency for the horse and as many of the other things as possible. We'll have you set up and ready to go by tomorrow.''

Lacy had a sudden dip in confidence. ''What if there isn't a story with this man? I mean, what if he's just an ordinary guy?''

Erin walked around the desk. Her face was stern. ''I've just dropped ten thousand dollars. Five for your advance and five for expenses. I don't want you to even consider that there isn't a story. All I can say is, if you can't find one, I hope you have a lively imagination.''

Lacy nodded. She understood perfectly. She would return with a story no matter what.

TURNER PUT THE CANNED GOODS on the old scarred counter and waited for the clerk to finish stocking the top shelf. The clerk was a hefty man with a white handlebar mustache and red cheeks.

"Looks like you're new around these parts," the man said as he rang up the goods and put them in a brown paper bag. "If you come back down this way, would you bring the bag back?"

"Sure," Turner said. "I'm for recycling."

"Recycling hell," the clerk said with a laugh. "I don't want to have to drive into town and buy more bags. Make 'em last as long as I can."

Turner nodded. "Do you have any D-size batteries?"

The clerk's eyebrows furrowed. "Dang it! Sold the last of them this morning to two guys. Came in here and 'bout wiped me out of ever'thing, as you can see." He frowned. "I asked 'em what they were huntin', but they said some foolishness. They were an odd twosome. I can't think of a critter that's in season right now."

Turner didn't like hunters in general and out-of-season hunters in particular. They had a million excuses about thinning herds and saving animals from starvation, but it all came down to plain bloodlust.

"What about some kerosene?"

The clerk hurried around the counter and came back with a five-gallon can. "I guess you know this stuff is dangerous."

Turner nodded. "I'd prefer a generator and electricity, but I don't know how long I'll be hanging around. I'll get by with some kerosene lamps for a while.''

"What are you huntin'?'' the clerk asked.

"Ever heard of a white panther in these parts?''

The clerk's eyes widened. "A white panther. You don't say. That's exactly what those other men were hunting. I thought they were pulling my leg.''

Turner was instantly alert. "They actually said they were hunting a white panther?''

"Yeah, they were laughin' about it. That's why I thought they were teasin' me. They said it had been spotted, and they were gonna kill it, skin it and sell the head and paws for trophies. They were sayin' how they could make at least a hundred thousand dollars.'' He tugged at his mustache. "So they weren't kiddin', huh? There is such a creature?''

Turner knew the sudden rage he felt had nothing to do with the clerk. His ire was directed at the two unnamed hunters. They had heard about a magical creature, a white panther that was reputed to have the power to change a person's life. And what was their reaction? They wanted to kill it and sell the body parts. It was incomprehensible.

"These two hunters, were they local men?'' he asked as nonchalantly as he could.

"No, sir. I know all the men in these parts. These were men from away. Not across the ocean or anything like that, but just not from around here at Crossroads.''

Turner debated how much to tell the clerk. "This white panther may be a myth. I track down myths, to prove or disprove them. But if there is such a creature here in Texas, it would be a shame if someone killed it.''

The clerk nodded. "Funny thing about some folks, whenever they see something of real beauty, their first impulse is to tear it down. Never understood that myself, but I see it all the time. Those two men, they were out to kill."

Turner paid for his supplies. "I'll be back and forth. I'd appreciate it if you could keep your ears open for me."

"Sure thing." The clerk looked over the purchases. "You don't need any ammunition?"

Shaking his head, Turner replied, "I don't carry a gun. Just a camera. My job is to document, not destroy."

"Well, that's a good way to look at life, but I'm tellin' you, mister, a gun can come in handy up in those hills. Sometimes it's a snake or something you can walk away from. Sometimes it's not. It's still a wilderness out there and you'd best use some caution."

Turner stuck out his hand and the men shook. "Thanks. I'll think about it, but for right now, I have more than I can pack up. Buster's tolerant, but he'll only put up with so much." He nodded to the horse tied up at the store rail.

"Goin' to the top?"

Turner liked the old clerk but not enough to reveal his destination. He'd learned to be cautious about telling anyone his plans or whereabouts, and he didn't want anyone to know he'd been living in an old abandoned cabin for the past two weeks. "I'll see how far I make it before nightfall."

"It's none of my business, but it can get mighty cold up there all of a sudden. It ain't winter yet, but I woke up this morning and felt Jack Frost blowing cold on my ankles. It won't be long before there'll be some snow. You got provisions?''

"Enough," Turner said evasively. "I'm well taken care of."

"Then you've got yourself some permanent shelter?"

Turner laughed. The clerk was a pretty damn good interrogator. "Did you ever work for the CIA?" he joked.

Turning red, the clerk laughed. "Sorry. Just a natural tendency toward nosiness. I do like to make sure folks know the score about those woods. I've been on a search party or two for some tenderfoots who went out there unprepared. They came back with very different attitudes."

"I'll bet." Being stranded in the wilderness would take the cockiness out of just about anybody.

Picking up his purchases, Turner started out the door. The clerk called him back. "Couldn't help but notice you didn't get any medicine."

"I'm not planning on being sick," Turner said.

The old man reached under the counter and brought out a small flask-size amber bottle. He walked up and stuck it in Turner's bag. "Just for medicinal purposes," he said, winking. "My daddy makes the stuff. He's eighty-six and never had a sick day in his life. Claims no germ can survive a good dose of this liquor. I don't like to sell it in the store—afraid I'll get caught. But it's genuine pure moonshine, and some of the best you'll ever taste. Have a sample on me."

"Thanks." Turner shifted the bag of goods so he could shake the man's hand again.

"Folks call me Melton," the clerk said. "Melton Weeks."

Turner introduced himself. He'd thought of using a false name, but it hardly seemed worth the effort. Crossroads, Texas, was a town so small he could almost spit across it. His reputation wouldn't follow him here. There would be no reporters, no gossip. Just his work.

"I'll keep you posted on what I hear about that white panther," Melton promised. "Think there might be a reward?"

Turner knew a good idea when he heard one. "Yes. There's a reward for information. A thousand dollars." He'd gladly pay that amount himself.

Melton's eyebrows lifted. "Just for information?"

Turner nodded. "And there's also another benefit. If you see the cat, your life will be changed."

"Changed how?" Melton was a little suspicious.

"For the better," Turner said with a grin. "According to the legend, any person who sees this cat will find themselves in a position to attain happiness."

"I don't suppose that goes for those two fellas who want to kill it."

"I don't suppose," Turner said. "No, those men aren't interested in happiness. They're only interested in money. This time, though, they may have bitten off more than they can chew."

Chapter Two

Lacy pulled the horse trailer into what passed for a parking lot beside the old store. Weeks Supply was the name on the faded sign, and she said a silent prayer that she wouldn't need supplies for an entire week. All she wanted was an interview, some photos and a straight road back to Dallas. The way she figured it, she could track Turner McLeod down in a day, spend the next day talking to him and be back at *Texas Legends* by midweek.

She got out of the truck and walked around the horse trailer to check on the big Appaloosa she'd rented from the Double O ranch in Comfort. The horse's name was Medicine Man, but he went by the nickname M&M. She could only hope he was as good as the candy. Slate and Cassidy, his owners, had promised he was sensible, sound and easy to love. So far, they hadn't fibbed.

"Easy, boy," she said as he fidgeted in the trailer. "We're almost there."

She walked up the steps to the store and opened the creaking screen. She had to use her shoulder to force the wooden door open—it was stuck in the jamb. When it did open, she stumbled inside and saw the look of amusement on the clerk's face.

"Howdy, little lady," he said, though she was five-nine and hadn't qualified as "little" since she'd hit a growth spurt in fourth grade.

"There wasn't a sign. Is this Crossroads?"

His white mustache twitched as he grinned. "The heart of town."

Lacy bit back a sarcastic comment. There was a bar, a mechanic, a gas station and this store. "I'm looking for directions to Finnegan's Point."

The clerk frowned. "You goin' up there alone?"

Lacy looked behind her. "I don't see anyone with me." She didn't mean to sound so snappy, but she was just a little bit scared, and she didn't need some stranger reinforcing her fears.

"Sorry, miss," he said contritely. "It's just that bad weather can spring up in the blink of an eye this time of year. Unless you're a seasoned camper, you might want to try for some place with easier access."

"I need to get to Finnegan's Point." She made herself sound firm.

He nodded. "Then you'll take the trail right behind the store and just follow it up." His eyes narrowed. "I'll risk getting' my head snapped off twice in a row by givin' you a little advice. It's a long trail, and there's nothin' up there but a few abandoned old homesteads, most of them pretty decrepit. I'd camp around here and set out in the mornin' if I was you."

Lacy pressed her lips together to stop the exclamation of dismay that almost escaped. Instead, she nodded. "Is it that long a ride?"

"About fifteen miles, and it's all steep and rocky. I hope you got a surefooted horse."

"I do," she said, even though she'd never ridden M&M. She thought again of the couple who owned M&M. They'd assured her he was steady and reliable. Their young daughter had ridden him.

The clerk leaned on the counter. "What's so interestin' up at the Point?"

Lacy debated on telling him the truth and finally decided it wouldn't hurt. "I'm looking for a man who investigates myths."

The clerk's face brightened. "That would be Mr. McLeod."

Lacy felt vast relief. "Yes, that's his name. Turner McLeod."

"Yeah, he was in here just this morning." He glanced at his wristwatch. "He's got about a three-hour lead on you, though. No way you can catch him today."

Disappointment made her frown. She shifted her weight from foot to foot. "But he is in these parts?"

"He's here. Now, findin' him out in that wilderness might be a chore."

"It isn't really all that bad," Lacy said. "Some of the terrain looks pretty steep, but it is classified as hill country."

The old man chuckled. "You can call it anything you want, but if you're aimin' to go out there, you might want to show it a little respect. Plenty of folks head out and don't make it, you know. Some of those ravines are mighty deep, and the trails can be treacherous, depending on the weather."

Lacy hadn't known that. Erin had told her that the terrain was rugged but easily hikable. Right.

"Mr. McLeod didn't lead me to believe he was expectin' any company," the clerk probed.

Lacy hesitated. "He isn't. I'm a magazine writer. I want to do a piece on his research."

"You mean that white panther?" The clerk's face livened at the mention of the big cat. "He said it was a legend. He said that if you saw the cat your life could be changed and you would find happiness."

Even though the story was likely a complete hoax, Lacy liked it. She'd first heard of the legendary cat as a child. She knew plenty about daydreams and fantasies that magically made life happy—she couldn't help smiling at the clerk's enthusiasm.

"Now you ought to smile more often, little lady," the clerk said approvingly. "When you get rid of that frown, you're a real knockout."

Instead of taking offense, Lacy actually smiled wider. Growing up, she'd enjoyed the compliments of her family and friends. She'd been considered a pretty girl, and her mother had occasionally talked about a modeling career for her. That was until her mother's death, until Lacy had been left as the only adult to care for her younger brother and sister. Then the dreams of a life of glamour had quickly fled before the reality of earning a living as a hairstylist. Ten-hour days of standing on her feet had knocked a lot of foolishness out of her.

"Thanks, Mister—"

"Weeks. Melton Weeks." He grinned. "Take my advice, little lady. Stay here for the night. You can take the storeroom if you want. I've got to head home to the missus, but nobody will bother you here."

There really didn't appear to be any other place to stay in Crossroads, unless she wanted to sleep on the ground. Which she didn't.

"That's mighty generous of you."

He shrugged. "We don't get a lot of visitors here, especially not ones as pretty as you. I'd worry all night if you headed out now. Stay the night, get a start at first light, and you might catch up with Mr. McLeod by tomorrow afternoon."

"Did he happen to say where he was staying?" Lacy asked.

"Nope. He was pretty closemouthed about his business all around. But he's up there huntin' that panther. There'll be tracks for you to follow. No chance of rain tonight, so they'll still be there in the mornin'. Just saddle up and follow."

Lacy started to confess that the only thing she'd ever tracked was a FedEx package. But she held her tongue. Sometimes confessing to a weakness was an invitation for trouble. She liked the clerk, but she'd learned the hard way not to trust strangers.

"Are you sure it won't be an inconvenience for me to stay here?" The floor would be hard, but at least it was inside. "And what about my horse? I can't leave him standing in the trailer."

The clerk gave her a long look. "There's a corral out back, and some grain and hay. You'll need to take a little for the horse when you go up."

She nodded. "I suppose there is water?" She hated to sound so hesitant, but she was really just getting a grip on everything she needed.

"There're creeks." He came around the counter and walked to the front door and looked out. "That your pickup?"

"It's a rental. Like the trailer."

"And the horse?"

She nodded.

"How much horseback ridin' you done?"

"I took lessons when I was a teenager. I can ride."

He didn't say a word, just kept looking out into the parking lot. "Why don't I help you unload the horse and settle him in? Then we can move the trailer around back and you can park it here."

Lacy felt ashamed of her earlier snippiness. "You're being more than kind."

He didn't respond. "Let's get that boy out of the trailer. I'll bet he's more than ready to stretch his legs."

Lacy followed Melton out and watched as he expertly brought M&M out. The horse looked around, then docilely followed Melton to the corral behind the store.

"At least you got a good horse," he said. "This boy can take you up to Finnegan's Point."

"How do you know?" Lacy asked, curious.

Melton turned around, his hand on the horse's withers. "He's lookin' around and takin' it all in. He's getting' his bearin's so he can get back here if he needs to."

"He'll remember how to get back here?" Lacy was impressed.

"You bet. If you get in trouble, just hang on in the saddle and let the horse have his head. He'll bring you back down."

"That's a good thing to know," Lacy said, feeling a little more confident about the entire adventure.

Melton helped her settle in before he left. Lacy found herself on a cot in the storeroom in the back of the store, a paperback novel in her hand. It was not how she'd expected to spend the night. She'd figured on being at Turner McLeod's campsite with her interview well under way.

Things just weren't going the way she'd planned.

TURNER BUILT A FIRE in the wood-burning stove and settled back in bed to watch the flames. Fire. He was both drawn and repelled by it. Since his teenage years, he'd had an intimate acquaintance with the horror of fire. That was when his younger brother, Benjamin, had died in a fire. Even now, some twenty years later, the thoughts of his brother made his bones feel stuffed with misery. Benjamin had been the kind of kid that everyone adored—a bright vivacious boy who loved sports and music and school. He'd had dozens of friends, all different kinds of people. And he'd died a terrible death because Turner had been unable to get down the hallway to his room and save him.

Turner felt Rex's cold nose in his palm, and he leaned down to pet the dog. Rex was one of those animals who knew when his master was taking a wrong path in his thoughts. Always after the dream, though, Turner had to go back to the beginning, back to the first fire, and then relive them all.

He'd had nothing to do with any of the fires. His only connection was that he'd been in the vicinity, and he'd known the people whose property had burned.

And he'd known Lilith. He closed his eyes against the memories that sprang unbidden into his mind. With her dark curly hair that hung almost to her waist and her brown eyes that seemed to catch the light and give it back, she was the most alive woman he'd ever known. And she'd loved him. Even though she'd ultimately rejected him, Turner didn't doubt her love. Something had happened, and if Lilith had lived, he would have figured out what it was and made it right.

But the fire had ended all his hopes and dreams. Now there was only the work.

To that end he got out of bed and went to a stack of books beside the wall. Gathering several into his arms, he returned to bed and continued with his research on the myth of the white panther.

The legend dated back to the early history of the United States, back to a time when Texas was still part of Mexico and the Apache rode the ranges and took shelter in the rough terrain of the hill country.

The panther was a totem animal, one of great power. Turner knew the similar legend of the white buffalo, an animal that Native Americans believed would mark the beginning of the fulfillment of tribal predictions mostly centered around peace and a resurgence of respect for Native American values. Such a creature had been born only a couple of years before. Turner hadn't investigated that particular legend, because he preferred the wilderness. The buffalo had been born in captivity, and Turner sought the solitude of the woods. No, the white panther was more his style.

The legend itself—that a sighting of the unusual cat would bring happiness to the viewer—gave him particular pleasure. It was a legend that required no heroics, no derring-do. And the blessing could be visited upon anyone who saw the elusive cat.

When Rex nuzzled him again to be let out, Turner knew it was time to go to bed. Rex had the best alarm clock in the world. He knew when it was time for him to go out and patrol the area, checking to make sure Buster was okay in his small corral and all the wild creatures of the woods knew that Turner and

Buster were under the dog's protection. Turner had learned a lot about animal communication in the past two years. Both Rex and Buster had taught him.

He put his books away and considered walking outside, but the night had grown cold. Inside the cabin the fire had made the air toasty warm, and he gave in to the urge to simply crawl into bed.

He was about to drift off to sleep when he heard Rex. The dog made a terrible racket, barking and growling fiercely. Turner was on his feet and dressed in an instant. He thought of Melton Weeks's advice that he needed a weapon, and he regretted being so hardheaded about it. A shotgun would have given him a lot more security than the piece of firewood he picked up.

Moving swiftly to the window, he listened for any unnatural sounds. Rex had fallen silent, but when he began to bark again, the dog was just outside the front door. Turner peered into the night. The trees hugging the small cabin were so thick he couldn't begin to examine the area with any real hope of seeing anything. He listened intently, trying to hear what had set Rex off.

For a long moment there was nothing, then the sound of Buster beginning to run. Rex barked again, this time a sharp savage bark of warning.

Turner pushed open the glass and leaped out the window into the freezing night. Country-savvy people would never approach another man's campsite—or cabin—in the middle of the night without giving some kind of warning. It was customary to call out, or the natural assumption was that whoever was out there was up to mischief.

Moving through the darkness with a great degree

of grace and agility, Turner slipped into the fringe of trees that marked the perimeter of the property. The intruder would think that Turner was still inside, so he would have the advantage of surprise. And he was going to need it if the intruder was armed.

Turner caught only a flash of movement—someone or something running away. Whoever or whatever it was darted into the thick underbrush. There was the sound of bushes and leaves being crushed and pushed aside, and Rex was on the heels of the intruder, barking like mad.

After listening for a moment, Turner stood up and walked across the clearing and back to the front door of the cabin. In a few moments Rex joined him.

"Good work," Turner said, patting the dog. "Now if only you could tell me who or what it was."

Rex wagged his tail and followed Turner into the house. Reclining on the bed once again, Turner thought about what had happened. In the morning he'd check the area for tracks. It could have been an animal, but Turner didn't think so. It hadn't moved like an animal, and Rex was too intent on protecting Turner and Buster to spend his doggy energy chasing a wild creature.

He stroked the dog's head and eased into sleep, hoping that he wouldn't dream again of fire.

"DANG IT!" Lacy tried tying the girth in a knot, only to discover that the leather slipped as soon as she put her foot in the stirrup. In the English saddles on which she'd learned to ride, the girths had buckles. She'd never tried to cinch a Western girth.

"At the risk of soundin' chauvinistic, let me give you a hand."

She turned to find an amused Melton Weeks standing in the back door of the store watching her. "I could use some help," she said with a wry grin. "I should have asked Slate how these things worked."

Melton ambled over and showed her the in-and-over tie that cinched the saddle securely in place. "It's not hard if you know how to do it," he said easily. "But it's hard to figure out on your own."

"Thanks for the help and for trying to keep me from feeling stupid," Lacy said. She brushed a lock of straight blond hair out of her eyes.

"I'd say you learned to ride English," Melton said. "Different tack. No reason to feel dumb because you don't know Western."

Lacy felt a genuine affection for the clerk. She'd woken up feeling more inadequate than she had on the day of her first college class. It had taken every bit of her courage to walk into that brick building and find a seat in a classroom where the majority of students were nearly a decade younger than she was. This writing assignment was making her feel the same way. But she knew she couldn't back down, just as she couldn't have walked away from an education. It was a necessary experience, and one she intended to turn to her advantage.

"Mr. Weeks, I see the trail." She pointed to a narrow pathway that led into the wild terrain. "Do I just follow it?"

"Call me Melton, please, and you can follow the trail pretty much up to the Point. But I'm not certain where Turner went. He might have gone to the Point or he might be camping somewhere off the trail. He seemed like a man who likes his privacy, so my best guess is, he's somewhere near the trail but not on it."

Lacy nodded. Melton's assessment of her quarry was pretty much right on target. He was a man who sought solitude.

"You got supplies?"

Lacy nodded. Thank goodness Cassidy had taken her in hand and helped pack her gear. "I'm good for three or four days."

Melton nodded. "If you don't come down by Thursday, I'm gonna worry."

Lacy was touched by his concern. She put a hand on his shoulder. "If I don't come down by Thursday, I *want* you to worry. And send in the National Guard."

Melton laughed. "A posse, too."

"Thank you." She swung up into the saddle and gathered the reins. "I'm sure I'll be fine."

"You will." Melton's face reflected only a little doubt. "Turner is mounted, of course. Just follow the hoof prints and if you feel uncomfortable, come on back. Could be I can find one of the local men to take you up there."

Lacy shook her head. "I'll manage just fine." She squeezed M&M with her legs and the gelding moved forward. Lacy didn't know Turner at all, but she felt it was best if she showed up alone. Turner wasn't going to welcome *her,* much less her and a guide.

The terrain was rocky and sun-blasted, but Lacy found a strange beauty in it. Dallas was so flat, so much asphalt and concrete, that she felt now as if she was in a foreign land. The hill country around Kerrville was gentler than around Crossroads. The Kerrville area consisted of flat plains and the quick rise of hills characterized the land. Here, though, the inclines were sharper and the declines descended into gulches that were prone to flash flooding during the rainy season.

Cedars grew everywhere, along with cottonwoods and some oaks. But it was the underbrush she watched. There were thistles with thorns sharp enough to penetrate M&M's hide—and her jeans.

She also kept one eye on the ground for the tracks she had to follow. They were sporadic but easy enough to spot where Turner's horse had stepped into a bit of sand. Even on the hard shale were places where she could see the horse had been. So far, tracking wasn't as difficult as she'd feared.

As she settled into the saddle and M&M's easy gait, she found her shoulders loosened and her hips began to swing with the motion of the horse. The Western saddle was comfortable, secure. It had been a long long time since she'd ridden. She'd given it up because it was a hobby her parents couldn't afford. Funny how she'd made herself forget how much she loved it.

Once she was established at the magazine and got a regular paycheck, maybe she'd have enough money to take riding lessons again. This time it would be…cutting. Or maybe barrel racing. After all, Texas was the home of the cowboys. Or just trail riding. Anything to be out in the fresh air and on a horse.

She stopped for lunch beside a small creek, allowing M&M to graze on the last of the grass. The temperature was perfect, a fall day that would leave the weathermen with nothing much to say. She finished her sandwich, rolled up her litter and put it in her saddlebag. Although she'd taken to riding again, her backside was still a little out of practice. She shifted on the ground, trying to find a soft spot in the grass.

By the time she found Turner, she was going to be really, really saddle sore. It was a fact she might be able to work to her advantage. If he took pity on her, he might not throw her out so fast.

She eased around for a more comfortable position as she smiled at the thought. It was a good fantasy, but only a fantasy. After reading the file on Turner, she knew he wasn't the kind of man who felt strong and masculine only when a woman showed her weakness. No, that kind of manipulation wouldn't work on him at all.

She'd given it some thought and she'd decided that her best approach was simply to tell him the truth. That she desperately needed the story and that she'd write the truth, not exaggerating any of it. *Texas Legends* had a reputation for highlighting the sensational over the factual, but she would make sure that her story was accurate. If she could convince Turner she'd be fair, he might welcome the chance to tell his side of the story.

There had been a photo of Turner in his file. He was a dark, handsome man with compelling eyes. From what she'd read in the file, there was no physical evidence to connect Turner to any of the fires. In two of them, he'd lost people he cared about—his brother and the woman he'd asked to marry him. It was true that Lilith Ascenti had first accepted and then rejected Turner's proposal of marriage. But few men were driven to burning a woman to death simply because she wouldn't marry him.

Closing her eyes, Lacy let her tired muscles relax. Beside her, M&M cropped the grass in a sound that was soothing and strangely familiar. In the first fire connected with Turner, his brother had died. Then there had been a fire in a small town where Turner lived. A garage had burned. The worst fire was Lilith Ascenti's house. The young woman had died in the blaze, even though all the windows in the house had been open.

Not in a single case was there a stitch of evidence to tie Turner to the fires. Still, the idea that he'd somehow started the fires followed him from town to town like a curse.

Lacy didn't believe in spontaneous combustion or that any human being had the power to magically think a fire into existence. But after reading the file, she was interested enough to want to know Turner's side of the story. And it would make a great magazine piece—one good enough for the cover.

Suddenly M&M stiffened and stopped eating. She rose on one elbow and looked around, the hair at the back of her neck rising. Someone was watching her— she could feel the gaze. Very slowly she got to her feet. Pretending a calm she didn't feel, she checked the girth on the saddle and made sure it was tight. M&M was steady as a rock, but his ears were pricked forward and he was staring intently at a copse of cottonwoods farther upstream.

"Hey, anybody here?" she called on the off chance Turner had stopped along the trail for something. It would work to her benefit if she found him so quickly.

There was no answer.

"Hello!" she shouted. "Mr. McLeod! Is that you?"

Again, only silence. Lacy swung up into the saddle. "Time to move on, M&M," she said softly to the horse as she nudged him away from the creek and back to the trail. Whether it was a bear, a deer, an armadillo or a human, Lacy didn't want a confrontation. She'd had her lunch and it was time to move along.

Even as she rode away, she could feel someone's gaze drilling a hole in her back. She wanted to turn around, but she didn't. She was just a little afraid of what she might see.

Chapter Three

Turner finished his coffee and set the small cabin in order, restacking his books and neatly pulling the quilts up on the bed. He wasn't really concerned about the tidiness of the place, but he'd found that by ordering his surroundings he was better able to order his thoughts. He was also waiting for full light before he went out to check the tracks around the cabin. The episode of the night before still troubled him.

Rex was at his side when he went outdoors. He gave Buster some grain and then walked toward the southwest corner of the cabin where Rex had gone after the intruder.

The first thing he saw was several small limbs snapped at shoulder height, but it was a good twenty yards into the woods before he found the first footprint. Looking down at it, he felt as if a cold wind had whistled down the neck of his jacket. The print was human and male—a large male, judging from the width of the sole and the depth of the indention in the sand. The treaded sole was worn, and Turner bent down to fully examine the track. It was possible that someone looking for a campsite had come upon the cabin and thought it was empty. That was the most likely explanation. What troubled Turner was that the intruder hadn't bothered to hail him or make any contact.

Turner stood up. He could follow the tracks, but he knew that whomever they belonged to was long gone. This time he'd chalk it up to a novice camper who didn't know the rules. This time. If it happened again, though, Turner was going to have to find out who was watching him. And why. In the past he'd learned the hard way that it was better to confront trouble head-on. Trying to ignore it or walk away from it was often the invitation for it to jump him.

He returned to the cabin and gathered his camera, binoculars and notes, and packed a lunch. From looking at the maps of the area, he'd discovered a cave about five miles away. Panthers were animals that liked a permanent den. The cave he'd read about would be perfect. And it was the only lead he had at the moment in his quest to find the white panther.

He saddled Buster, strapped on his gear and headed down the trail he'd taken the day before for supplies. There was a turnoff that would take him west into even rougher terrain. With Rex running alongside, Turner relaxed in the saddle and let the apprehensions of the morning slide away. Just because someone had stumbled onto the cabin he was using didn't mean problems were on the way. He had to keep his head clear and not borrow trouble.

With that in mind he began to whistle as he let Buster find the easiest route south. All around him nature was in the last preparations for the coming winter. He snugged up the collar of his jacket and pulled his hat lower over his eyes to cut the wind. The temperature was dropping every hour. Instead of getting warmer, the day was getting colder. To the east a bank of gray clouds was building.

"Looks like snow tomorrow," he said to the horse and dog. Rex barked and Buster completely ignored him.

When he finally reached the vicinity of the cave, he tied Buster's reins to a tree and ordered Rex to stay with the horse. Taking the camera and binoculars, he went on alone on foot. He didn't believe the cat would be in the cave—that would be too much luck for him. But he would check to see if there were indications that anything lived in the cave. He was looking for the bones of prey, spoor, the signs that would tell him the species that occupied the cave—and whether it was predator or game.

He was careful as he approached. Humans had their rules in the wilderness and most animals did, too. Large cats were seldom predatory toward humans. They attacked only when they felt threatened. Going into their home was a threatening action, and Turner was fully aware of it. There was no other choice, though, if he wanted to check for the cat.

He slipped into the narrow cave opening and let his eyes adjust to the darkness as much as possible. He'd brought a flashlight, and though he was reluctant to use it, he had to. The intense beam bounced around the cave, creating shadows that expanded and shrank as he shifted back and forth. The cave was deeper than he expected.

Moving very slowly and cautiously in case there was any animal in the cave, he eased deeper, aware that the floor sloped down, as if it led into the heart of the hillside. He shone the flashlight from side to side, exploring the rugged walls of the cave.

He'd proceeded a good fifteen yards before he could see the back wall of the cave. The map hadn't indicated that the space was so large, but time could have shifted the dimensions, or the person who'd recorded the cave might not actually have been inside it. No matter, the result was the same. There were no bones or any sign of a big cat living on the premises.

Turner wasn't disappointed. He hadn't actually expected to find the panther. That would have been too easy—and, he admitted to himself, he didn't want the search to end that quickly. After Christmas would be a good time to spot the cat. That way his quest would keep him occupied through that most difficult time of year.

He turned around to leave. There were other caves, crevices, washouts and a thousand other places a cat might want to make a lair. A lot depended on the gender of the animal—something he'd never been able to ascertain in his research. A female would look for security for her cubs, while a male would be more interested in the proximity of game. As he thought about the possibility of cubs, Turner smiled. That would be spectacular—to find not only the white panther, but a litter of cubs.

Turner started out of the cave with a lot more speed and a lot less caution than he'd used going in. He almost missed the pawprint in the soft dirt of the floor. After stumbling in his effort to avoid stepping on it, he swung the light down for a better look and felt his gut tighten. Together the pads measured better than five inches across, and there were four deep indentations where the animal's claws had gripped the soil. It was a big animal. Magnificently big.

Pulling out his camera, Turner photographed the

print, then quickly repacked his things. If a large cat *was* living in the cave, he didn't want to be there when the creature came home.

He went back to Rex and Buster, ate a late lunch and then decided to return to the cabin. He'd had some vague notion about scouting out another area, but the dropping temperatures made the idea of a longer ride unappealing—to him and to Buster. He wanted enough daylight to be sure Buster had plenty of hay and a good place to shelter out of the wind.

He let Buster take his time picking a path back to the trail. He was inordinately fond of Buster, a horse with plenty of sense. Unlike a lot of high-strung horses, Buster was reliable and unflappable— Turner managed to grab the saddle horn just as Buster shied abruptly sideways. Beside him, Rex wheeled and barked, and out of the corner of his eye, Turner caught sight of a spotted horse that came running hell-for-leather up the dangerously rocky trail.

Turner's gut contracted with the knowledge that someone was in trouble. The horse wore a saddle and bridle, and the reins dangled dangerously under the horse's feet as it charged toward him.

"Easy, fella," Turner said as he got off Buster and walked toward the obviously frightened animal. The horse's eyes showed white all around, and it jerked and quivered as Turner reached slowly toward it. With one smooth motion, he caught the reins and spoke softly to the trembling horse, soothing him with his voice and with a hand on his neck. "Easy, there, fella. Where's your rider?" He moved closer and saw the bloodstain that was still fresh on the horse's neck. He quickly checked to make sure the horse wasn't injured before he accepted the conclusion that the missing rider had been injured, perhaps seriously.

He looked down the trail, hoping that someone would come walking, a little bruised and bloodied but otherwise unhurt. The only thing on the trail was a rabbit that darted into the open, took one look at Rex and then beat a hasty retreat for its hole.

All thoughts of going home evaporated. There was no option. Turner knew he was going to have to find the missing rider—or spend the entire night hunting. With the weather getting colder and grayer by the minute, an injured person could easily die.

Leading both horses, he set off down the trail, his eyes roving the ground to make sure he was following the horse's trail back to the point where its rider had gone astray.

LACY KNEW THAT SOMETHING terrible had happened to her. She lay on the ground, feeling the cold creep from her feet up her legs and slowly over her torso. She was freezing, but every time she tried to sit up, the dizziness returned and she fainted. Although she was miserably cold, she decided to lie still for a few moments and see if she could regain her equilibrium.

She wasn't certain what, exactly, had happened. She and M&M had been coming up the trail when a man had stepped out of the underbrush. He'd been dressed in camouflage fatigues with a cap pulled low over his face. A dark beard had covered his jaw, and he'd moved so fast that Lacy, trying to handle the startled horse, hadn't had a chance to really look at him.

He'd made a grab for M&M's bridle as if he intended to restrain the horse. Instinctively Lacy had used her heels in the horse's side to keep him moving forward. She didn't want anyone grabbing the reins—and control of her horse. It was a definite act of aggression.

"Stand clear," she'd warned the man.

"What's a pretty little thing like you doin' out here alone in the woods?" the man had asked. He had a strange accent and a grin that made her entire body tighten with fear.

"Stand aside," she'd ordered, more firmly this time.

"Or what?" he'd asked menacingly.

"Or I'll hurt you," Lacy said clearly.

"Oh, now that scares me to death." The man had laughed and taken a step closer.

Lacy had had very little patience left—she'd about used it all up. After ten years of working in the hair salon and listening to women complain about the treatment they suffered at the hands of men, she was determinedly single and not about to let some man push her around.

The man had reached up and snatched the bridle just below the bit. Without thinking Lacy had kicked down on his arm with her booted foot. She hadn't broken his arm, but it wasn't because she hadn't tried. And that, she'd realized as she moaned on the ground in pain, had been her first mistake. She'd assumed that the guy would fight by the rules. It wasn't until she saw the look in his eyes that she'd realized he was without rules or principles. And she was alone with him.

Fear had made her really clap her heels into M&M's sides. The horse, restrained by the man's hand on his bridle, had had no where to go but up.

Lacy had stayed on M&M as he reared. She'd hoped the threat of M&M's heavy hoofs coming down on him would have sent the man running. To her amazement, he hadn't budged an inch. When M&M had regained all four feet, Lacy had felt the man's hand close around her lower thigh. His fingers had dug deeply into her muscle, and when she'd leaned down to try to pry his hand away, he'd punched her, hard. Blood had spurted from her lip, staining M&M's neck.

She'd been so surprised that she hadn't reacted. The pain had hit her face like a sledgehammer, and the man had taken advantage of her condition. Reaching up, he'd grabbed her long hair and swiftly jerked her from the saddle.

A burst of pain rocketed through her head as she struck a rock. She had come to consciousness only a few minutes ago to find her horse and all her gear gone, and her body throbbing in at least a dozen places.

She sat up again, this time determined to stand. She was freezing, and if she didn't get a move on, she'd have to sleep on the mountain without a blanket or any provisions. The sky was leaden, and it was at least ten degrees colder than it had been an hour earlier. The temperature was dropping at such a rapid pace it was frightening. The day had started out balmy and lovely. Now it looked as if God was about to unleash his wrath.

She managed to get to her hands and knees, and for a moment she held on to the hope that she would stand and then walk. M&M had to be around someplace. The horse was solid gold. After she'd hit the ground she had a vague memory of the man crying out in pain. M&M had tried to protect her. And now she wanted to know what had happened to her horse.

Remaining on all fours, she crawled toward a rock and felt queasy when she saw the blood. This was the rock her head had struck. Probing her scalp gently with the fingers of one hand, she found a gash just above her right ear. Her fingers moved over her face, finding dried blood. Luckily nothing felt broken, though her face seemed swollen to twice its normal size.

Her concern now, though, was M&M. Where was he? Was he injured? She had to find him and figure out a way to get back to civilization. Without blankets and camping gear, she'd freeze before dawn.

She crawled over to a tree and used the trunk to pull herself to her feet. The dizziness made her want to give up and sit down, but she locked her knees and gripped the tree with all of her strength. Counting her breaths, she ordered her body to calm, to hold tough. Amazingly it obeyed, and she felt her strength returning. The fall had stunned her, but she was at last getting her bearings back.

She let go of the trunk to see if she could balance. She took a few tentative steps, feeling stronger with each one.

She was standing tall when she heard someone coming down the trail. She didn't have the strength to run and hide, so she drew herself up to her full five foot nine and gritted her teeth to keep them from chattering.

The first thing to come into sight was a man dressed in jeans and a denim jacket with fleece lining. A hat was pulled low over his face and he walked with a casual swagger. Behind him was M&M. It wasn't the man who'd attacked her, but it had to be one of his cohorts. He had her horse!

"You dirty bastard." Lacy was no longer weak—she was furious. The man was acting as if he didn't have a care in the world. Well, she wasn't going to stand around and wait for another man to slug her. She launched herself across the rocky trail with the intention of doing as much bodily harm to him as possible. There really wasn't another choice, because she didn't have the energy or the wherewithal to get away from him.

"Wait just a minute!" The man held up a hand, but it was too late. Lacy couldn't stop her charge.

"You horse thief!" she cried, arms pummeling his shoulders and back as she leaned against him. "You low-life horse thief! I hope they still hang people like you in this state!"

She heard the chuckle even as she flailed away at the man. "Take it easy, ma'am. I found your horse running loose on the trail."

"I'm going to make you suffer!" She redoubled her efforts to slug him. He simply caught her wrists and held them until she lost what little strength she had.

"Lady, my patience is wearing thin. I suggest you hold still long enough to listen to me. I found the horse up the trail, and I came back here looking for the owner. You've been hurt, and I can't tell how badly with you jumping around all over the place."

Lacy found her hands restrained in an iron grip. She was panting and her face and head were throbbing as if Thor and his thunder hammer were working on her. "Give me the horse and let me go."

"Sure." She felt his hands loosen so fast she didn't

have time to recover her balance. She was falling, falling. Blue sky, green trees and the yellow-red earth whirled around her as she tumbled, then hit the ground so hard the wind was knocked from her lungs. Once again, pain was the last thing she remembered.

BY THE TIME Turner got back to the cabin, he was very worried about the young woman. She'd lain across the saddle of her horse, loosely tied into place for her own protection, as he'd taken her to his home—or what currently passed for a home. All the way he'd felt the black cloud of bad luck following him.

This woman was a stranger, and one who was mentally unbalanced if her actions were any clue. She'd attacked him as if he were Satan incarnate. All he'd been trying to do was return her horse and help her.

She was still out cold—and her face was a mess—as he lifted her off the saddle and carried her into the cabin. Her blond hair fell over his shoulder, and even with all the trouble she'd made for him, he couldn't help but smell the rain-fresh scent of her tresses. It was a scent from another life, when he'd taken pleasure in the ways of a woman. Lilith's hair had always smelled like flowers and rain, and one of his greatest pleasures had been feeling it brush across his naked chest in moments of passion.

He kicked the door open, more disturbed by his thoughts than with the woman he held in his arms. Standing in the doorway, he surveyed his abode. There was only one place to put her, and he did—on the bed. Even though he was irritated, his moves were gentle. He took great care not to jar her head, because he knew the cuts and bruises would be painful.

Outside the temperature continued to drop, and he went to the watering trough and got the first film of ice that had formed. Wrapping pieces of it in a cloth, he took the ice pack inside and placed it on her nose. The cold would help the swelling go down, and then he'd be able to tell more about the injury. The gash in her head wasn't serious, but might need stitches, but that was a little more than he'd bargained for. He could do it—but he wasn't certain she'd welcome the result. With her looks, she'd want a plastic surgeon.

He pushed the silky blond strands aside and took a closer look at the wound. It wasn't as deep as he'd first thought, but it did need cleaning. All in all, she was a mess.

He got up to find soap and to heat some water. Rex moved to the side of the bed and whined softly.

"Traitor," Turner said with a shake of his head. Even the dog thought she was pretty.

He gathered the things he needed and put them beside the bed. The afternoon light slanted in the window, and he worked with quick efficient movements. Living alone in the wilderness, he'd learned the necessary things about tending wounds. Still, the extraordinary feel of the woman's smooth skin beneath his hands was unsettling. Everything about her was unsettling. He couldn't wait for her to wake up so he could figure out a way to get her down the path to civilization and out of his hair.

At her first moan, he stopped cleaning her scalp. Even though she wasn't awake, she must have felt what he was doing and it hurt. No matter, it had to be done or she risked serious infection. He gave her a moment, then started again. When she opened her eyes and stared directly at him, he felt as if he'd been hit by a stun gun.

"What do you think you're doing?" she asked, but she didn't move.

"Lady, your head is hard, but somehow you managed to split it open. I'm trying to clean the grit and shale out of the wound in the hope it won't get infected."

He daubed at the wound again and saw her flinch. "Sorry," he said, "but you won't thank me if I stop."

"Go ahead," she said, pressing her lips firmly together, probably to stop her chin from trembling.

"Want a shot of whiskey?" he asked, suddenly remembering the stuff for "medicinal" purposes Melton Weeks had given him.

"And a bullet to bite?" the woman asked sarcastically. "No thanks. All I really want is my horse and directions back to that little supply store."

Turner lifted one eyebrow. "Good. I was afraid you'd say you were a relative of mine who'd come to visit. I'll get you cleaned up, and as soon as you're strong enough, I'll help you leave."

"Good," the woman said. She closed her eyes and endured the remainder of his medical attention.

"There you are," he said at last with more than a little satisfaction. "You could use stitches, but you won't die without them. Your nose is bruised but not broken and your lip is swollen. So what happened?"

Her blue eyes opened to stare into his. "I didn't fall."

"Then what happened?" Instead of picking up the medicine and putting it away, Turner found that he'd settled into his chair and was interested in hearing her answer.

"A man came out of the brush and grabbed my horse's reins. When I tried to get away from him, he punched me in the face and then pulled me from the saddle. I thought he was stealing M&M, my horse, until I saw that you had him."

"I see." He didn't show the woman how much her words concerned him. If what she said was true, a dangerous man was on the loose in the woods. He would have to escort the woman back down to the supply store. "And after attacking me and accusing me of horse theft, you now believe I didn't steal your horse."

"Now that I can see you, I know you're not the same man. You're Turner McLeod, aren't you?"

The disquiet he'd felt all day expanded. "How did you know that?"

The woman pushed herself up with her arms, suddenly seeming to realize she was in his bed. She blushed a furious red but didn't complain. "I'm Lacy Wade," she said, extending her hand. "I'm here to talk to you about a magazine piece."

If she had said she was there to rob him, beat him and leave him for dead, Turner could not have gotten angrier. He stood up so fast he spilled the basin of water he'd used to clean her wounds.

"You're out of here, lady."

"Look, this isn't the kind of story that you think. I want to write—"

"I don't give a damn what you want to write. I don't talk to reporters."

"I'm not a reporter. Not technically. I'm a—"

"You're gone is what you are." He strode over to

the window and looked out. "Damnation!" he thundered. "It's snowing!" He whirled around in time to see the look of satisfaction on her face. That made him even angrier. He strode up to the bed and leaned down. "You may think you've played this pretty smart, but it won't get you anywhere. I don't have a choice but to let you stay tonight. In the morning, though, you're going back to Weeks Supply and what you do from there, I don't really give a damn. But you'll go back, and you'll go back without a story!"

Chapter Four

After the first hour, Lacy felt as acutely uncomfortable as she had when she first walked into that college classroom at the age of thirty. Turner McLeod made it abundantly clear he didn't want her within a hundred miles of him. For the most part, he made ignoring her a science.

Four times he'd brought in ice from outside to put on her nose, and he'd checked her forehead to see if she was running a fever. His touch had been gentle, but there had been no hint of friendliness in his blue eyes. He kept his broad shoulders turned away from her as much as possible, leaving her to notice his lean, muscular build. His dark hair needed a trim, but she couldn't help but notice how thick it was. His handsome looks, though, were offset by his unapproachable attitude. If the weather hadn't been so bad, she was sure he would have risked a nighttime trip down to the supply store just to get rid of her. Well, she hadn't asked to be attacked and injured, and she hadn't even considered that it might snow. None of this was her fault. Technically.

Still lying on his bed, she watched as he brought

in another armload of wood from outside. A flurry of snow blew in with him, and she shivered.

"I've never seen a snow set in so early here," he said. "Luckily it looks like it won't last. By the time the sun really gets up tomorrow, it'll be gone. Maybe sooner." It was the first halfway-civil statement he'd made since she'd revealed she was a writer.

"It's hard to believe that I was wearing a sleeveless dress in Dallas." She struggled to find something to say that wouldn't annoy him—and then ended up sounding shallow and foolish. The truth was, the hardest thing to believe was that she was in a strange man's bed in a cabin in the middle of nowhere. That was definitely something she didn't want to say.

Turner stacked the wood. "I knew a front was coming in, but it sure blew up in a hurry."

She looked around for a radio or some means of communication. "How did you know?"

"Experience," he said without a hint of amusement. "You stay up here long enough and you learn to pay attention to the trees and the birds. My dog and horse, too. They know when the weather's changing."

"Have you lived around here long?" she asked.

The muscle in his jaw tensed. "Lady, let's stick to the weather. It won't matter if I'm misquoted on that."

It was the final straw. Lacy swung her feet to the floor and stood up. The dizziness was like a wall, but she locked her knees and rode it out. Like the queasiness, it passed after a moment.

"I'm not staying here," she said, walking over and picking up her coat. "Where's my horse and saddle?"

Turner stood with his hands on his hips, blocking

the doorway. "Your horse and saddle are out in the shed, but you aren't leaving here at this time of night in this weather. In case you haven't noticed, it's snowing outside, and it's dark."

"I've noticed. I've also noticed what a jackass you are. I didn't get hurt deliberately, and I was coming up here to talk to you without suspecting that I'd be your guest. You've made it clear that you don't want me here, and I'm ready to go."

He looked at her for a moment. "Is it pride that's talking?"

His question only made her angrier. "You're damn right it's pride. I worked my butt off to get a college education, and this is my first chance at a job as a writer. I don't have to tell you how hard I worked, and now I have a chance to get something I want in my life, and you're acting like I'm some kind of pond scum. I can't change your opinion, but I don't have to stay here and have it shoved down my throat." She reached for her jacket and slipped into it.

"Look, Lacy—"

"My name is Ms. Wade. Only my friends call me Lacy."

"Ms. Wade, would you settle down long enough to listen to me?"

She glared at him, trying to determine if he was mocking her. "Listen to what? More grousing and snapping? Forget it."

He advanced a step toward her, shrugging out of his jacket as he did so. He slung the jacket over the back of a chair and fed several sticks of firewood into the old stove.

"Not even an experienced woodsman could make

it down the trail tonight. I promise to take you down tomorrow, when it will be safe for both of us.''

"I'm not staying here and listening to you—"

"Until tomorrow, I promise not to say anything else about your chosen career.'' He held up a hand. "Not a single word. I promise.''

Lacy looked past him to the window. Outside it was as black as the center of a well, and the snow sporadically fluttered against the pane. As mad as she was, she realized that she wouldn't last ten minutes on her own. The best thing would be to give in gracefully. "I don't have much of a choice,'' she said. "And neither do you, I suppose,'' she conceded. "We'll call a truce.''

"Agreed,'' he said. "The horses are safe, and I'm going to make some supper. How does a Spanish omelet sound?''

Lacy realized she was starving. "Perfect.'' She hesitated. He was so touchy. "I can help,'' she said. "My brother says I make the best biscuits in Texas.''

Turner's smile was so tentative it was barely there. "I haven't had homemade biscuits in about...'' The smile faded. "In a long time. If you're up to it, I'll get the ingredients.''

Lacy studied his back as he brought out the supplies. He'd been about to smile—and then something had triggered a memory. Something unpleasant that had to do with...biscuits? Or perhaps with someone who made them. Maybe the woman he'd been engaged to in Louisiana. The one who'd died in a fire. Lacy had done her research and put the scant pieces of information she could find together. The picture that came up made her keep her comments—and her questions—to herself.

As she mixed the biscuits, Turner prepared the ingredients for the omelet. It was a simple meal, but she found her mouth watering in anticipation. She was starving.

"We should be ready to eat in about ten minutes," Turner said. "Thanks for your help."

"I've never actually baked in a wood stove," Lacy said. "My great grandmother used to tell stories about the days when she could cook for her family and ten ranch hands. Of course, that was back before they lost the ranch during the Depression."

Turner put coffee cups on the narrow table beside the bed. "I used to hear the same kinds of stories. Only it was my grandfather, and he would talk about repairing fences during blizzards and birthing calves with the river flooding and a tornado on the horizon."

Outside the wind howled, but inside the cabin it was warm. The smell of the food was tantalizing, and Lacy sat on the edge of the bed and watched Turner put the finishing touches on the meal. At least they'd found a topic they could talk about with some degree of pleasantness. The distant past seemed a safe enough subject.

"My grandmother Alice was fourteen when the worst of the Depression hit her family. She married when she was fifteen. She learned to read when she had her first baby so she could read to my mom. A neighbor lady taught her."

"Sounds like she was a determined woman."

"She was," Lacy agreed. "Folks say I'm a lot like her."

"How so?"

"Hardheaded."

Turner actually smiled as he put the plates of omelet and hot biscuits on the narrow table. "Just keep your seat and I'll take the chair."

Lacy didn't wait for a second invitation. She picked up her fork and took a bite of the omelet. "This is good," she said. "Spicy. You have this place pretty well supplied. You must have made a lot of trips down to the store."

"I've spent a lot of time in various kinds of camps. The secret is to use everything you pack. It's not hard to bring up a jar of pimentos or some spices, as long as they aren't dead weight. You have to use them."

Lacy looked around the cabin. "I wouldn't exactly call it homey, but it beats sleeping on the hard ground." The minute she said it, she felt the blush creep up her cheeks. There was only one bed, and if she slept in it, then Turner would have to take the floor.

"In my line of work, you learn to make do without too many luxuries." His smile was wry. "And tonight I'll take the floor."

"Absolutely not. I'll take the floor. It's not exactly like I'm an invited guest."

Turner's smile lifted at one corner. "Invited or not, you'll take the bed. The issue is settled."

Lacy started to say something else, then took another bite of food. Arguing with Turner McLeod was like throwing rocks at the moon. No matter how good her aim might be, it didn't matter. She'd take the bed and get on her way in the morning, just as soon as there was enough light to see. As for the magazine article, it would nearly kill her, but she was just going to have to tell Erin Brown she hadn't been able to get the interview.

"What part of Texas are you from, Dallas?" Turner asked.

She was surprised that he was making a further attempt at conversation. "No, near Austin, though I didn't make it into the city all that much. It's a little town called Merryville. I grew up there."

"Small towns are good places to grow up. Must be a pretty handy place to learn to make biscuits, too. These are excellent."

Lacy found that when Turner smiled, he was a completely different man. Gone was the exterior that reminded her of a rock wall. There was even a twinkle in his blue eyes.

"My grandmother taught me before she passed away. I guess I've been making biscuits since I was about six."

"That's getting an early start."

"I always enjoyed breakfast." It was true. The long years of taking care of her brother and sister had contained moments of pleasure and joy. Breakfast had been a time for the three of them to talk, before the day got so busy that they seemed to be running around each other.

"I like the mornings, too," Turner said. "New day, fresh start—anything is possible early in the morning."

Lacy took another bite of omelet. She looked at him from under lowered lids. He was a good-looking man, something she hadn't expected. She'd seen pictures of him, but none of them captured the rugged handsomeness that showed up in the crinkles beside his eyes or the one-cornered lift of his smile.

They finished the meal in an easy silence, and Lacy

rose to clear the table. "If you'll tell me where, I'll wash these up," she said.

Turner walked to the window and looked outside. "The good news is that it's stopped snowing. The bad news is that washing up and other...necessities are done outside. There's a privy."

Lacy could easily imagine the cold sweep of the wind, but she was determined to do her share of the chores. "Point me in the right direction," she said.

Turner was smiling as he handed her his jacket. "It's warmer than yours. Are you sure you're up to this?"

"I insist," she said.

"Somehow I'm not surprised."

She looked up to see amusement on his face, but this time it had a softer edge. He wasn't mocking her, just teasing her a little.

"I suggest we wait until morning," Turner said.

"Best to get the kitchen clean before we go to bed," Lacy said. She'd learned the importance of keeping up with cleaning.

Turner's lopsided smile lifted one corner of his mouth once again. "I won't argue with you. The creek's to the left, and the outhouse is in the same direction. I could go with you and carry the light."

She shook her head. The last thing she wanted was Turner hovering around with a light while she took care of business.

It wasn't until she stepped into the night that she learned how dark it could be without a single street-light around. The night had a density that was almost physical. The storm clouds were blowing through, and high above the trees a half-moon winked. Lacy held the dishes in one hand, a flashlight in the other.

It would have been best to wait until daylight to wash the dishes as Turner recommended, but now she'd said she was going to do it. She wouldn't give him the satisfaction of seeing her turn tail and go back inside.

Picking out the path with the flashlight, she made her way to the creek. The water was like liquid ice as she rinsed the dishes. She wasn't certain they were spotless, but they were clean enough, she decided as she stacked them, ready to hurry back toward the cabin and the warm fire.

She was standing up when the snap of a branch caught her attention. She froze. Someone, or something, was watching her. She could feel it.

Her first impulse was to call out, but she didn't. She remembered the man who'd attacked her. Still holding the dishes, she snapped off the flashlight and began to back down the trail toward the cabin.

Another noise came from her right, this time a little closer. Her heart pounded so loudly she was afraid whoever was watching her would hear. Step by step she moved toward safety—toward the cabin and Turner.

The light from the window was like a beacon as she moved sideways toward it, one eye on the path behind her. A sudden movement deep in the underbrush was the final straw. Abandoning the dishes without a second's thought, she ran the final twenty-five yards to the door of the cabin and burst through it.

"There's someone out there," she said to a startled Turner. "Watching me. They were watching me."

Turner took the light from her hand and went to the door.

''Aren't you taking a gun?'' she asked. She looked around for a weapon.

''I don't have one,'' Turner said. ''My line of work doesn't normally attract a criminal element. It isn't like working for a tabloid where almost everyone wants to kill you.''

She didn't have a chance to respond before he was out the door and gone into the night.

TURNER REGRETTED his words as soon as they were out of his mouth. He'd made a promise not to say anything more about her job, and he'd broken his word.

Worse, he'd laid the blame for a possible intruder at her door, and he wasn't at all certain she deserved it. Someone had been nosing around the cabin before she arrived.

It was just that Lacy was in his space. He'd gotten used to being alone, and now, suddenly, there was a woman. And a good-looking one, too. Even though she was a reporter, she had a pleasing attitude and determination to do her share. She'd gone out to wash the dishes when most other women would have backed off. Even when she was outside, he'd thought about her. And a few of the thoughts that had popped into his head had been disturbing. He'd found himself wondering what it might be like to kiss her. And that was forbidden territory. Fate had given him a solitary life, and every time he'd thought to change that, tragedy had struck. He wasn't falling for heartache and disaster again. Unfortunately, he'd snapped at Lacy because he couldn't control his own fantasies.

He put his thoughts aside as he got closer to the creek. All of his attention was on the woods around him. Had she really heard something, or had the absolute darkness of the woods spooked her?

Rex was beside him, and the big dog began to growl. Turner put a restraining hand on the dog's neck. He didn't want Rex tangling with a wildcat or a man with a gun. Rex, when necessary, could be a ferocious animal, but he was no match for claws or bullets.

In the corral the horses snorted and began to run. Turner held himself perfectly still. Something was out in the night. Whether it was human or beast, he didn't know.

He had the flashlight, but he chose not to use it. His night vision was keen, and he knew that if he turned the light on, he'd be a perfect target. If someone was out there.

Buster gave a shrill call, and Turner's uneasiness increased. He began to move toward the corral. The moon broke through the clouds, and he saw the two horses wheeling and running, but could detect nothing else around the wooden fence.

With Rex beside him, sniffing and growling, he walked the perimeter of the shed and corral and found no sign that anyone had been near the animals. When it was daylight, he'd come back out and check more closely.

"Easy, fellas." He slipped under the railing and went to soothe the horses. As soon as he was beside them, they settled down. He waited until they went back to nibbling the hay he'd put out for them, then he headed to the cabin.

Lacy was sitting on the bed when he and Rex went inside. He'd decided that the best way to approach Lacy was directly. What surprised him was that she looked so upset. His remark had truly hurt her feelings.

"I didn't find anything out there," he said. "I'll check more thoroughly tomorrow." He decided against telling her about the previous incident.

"Thanks for looking. I left the dishes outside," she said.

"They'll be there in the morning. Don't worry about it." He hesitated. "Look, I'm tired and it's late. I apologize for that remark about the tabloids. It was out of line and I shouldn't have said it. Now let's go to bed."

He didn't give her a chance to argue. When he blew out the two lanterns, the cabin was in absolute darkness. He used his jacket as a pillow and found a place on the floor as far from her as he could. He was both satisfied and annoyed that she made no attempt to talk to him.

Turning on his side, he let the long day pull him into sleep.

LACY STARED UP at the ceiling, or at least where she thought the ceiling was. It was so dark in the cabin that if she got out of bed, she'd trip and kill herself.

She'd been ready to jump Turner when he'd come back in the door. His apology, delivered more as a threat than anything else, had taken the wind out of her sails. At least he recognized that he'd made a mistake. She knew a lot of people who wouldn't admit to being wrong—ever.

But she was going to have to admit it. To Erin Brown. She cringed as she imagined the conversation. *Texas Legends* had fronted the money for her expedition based on her promise that she would get the story of Turner McLeod. She'd rented a truck, trailer and horse, and bought a lot of expensive equipment all on the magazine's tab. Erin had been generous, because she wanted this story. So far all Lacy had gotten was a bruised face, a gash in her scalp and a few biting remarks from her quarry.

This wasn't exactly a promising start to the writing career she'd envisioned for herself.

If she went back without the story, she'd be fired. Her first job as a writer would be over in less than forty-eight hours, and she'd be back in the hair salon. Great! She could almost smell the acrid solution used to perm hair.

She shifted in the bed, trying to find a position that would shut off her brain so she could sleep. She was facing Turner when she heard him say something.

At first she wasn't certain, but then he spoke again, this time distinctly.

"Lilith, come out!"

The passion in the words made Lacy hold her breath.

"Lilith, come out of there!"

There was suffering in his tone, as if he was watching something horrible.

"Lilith!" He thrashed violently.

Lacy wondered that he didn't wake himself up on the hard floor. He was moving as if he was struggling against someone or something.

"Lilith, you have to wake up!"

Lacy sat up in bed. She gripped the mattress with both hands. It was almost unbearable to listen to Turner. Whatever nightmare he was having, it was tearing him apart.

She slipped to the floor and crawled across the

cabin until she touched his leg. Moving up it, she found his chest, then his face. He was raging hot, as if he stood at the edge of a powerful blaze. But this fire was inside him, and Lacy wasn't certain what to do.

"Lilith!" He almost howled the name.

Her reaction was spontaneous. She lightly patted his cheek. "Turner, wake up."

He stilled beneath her hand, and she took a deep breath.

"Turner, wake up. You're having a nightmare."

She was completely unprepared for his hands. They clamped on her arms and pulled her down to his chest. Lacy was about to say something else when she felt his lips capture hers. The kiss was burning hot, an experience of such intensity that she forgot her bruised lip—forgot to pull away.

Turner pulled her down against him, rolling so that he was beside her, his lips still claiming hers.

Lacy put her hands against his chest. He was a strong man, whipcord lean and muscled. His kisses were deep and passionate, and against all rational thought, she felt herself begin to respond.

It wasn't until his hand slid up her side and captured her breast that she realized how quickly she'd lost control—of herself and the situation.

She pushed against his chest, signaling for him to stop. "Turner—"

"My God, I thought you were burning," he said softly. "I saw the flames."

"Turner?" Lacy felt the goose bumps dance over her entire body. Turner wasn't awake. He was kissing her and thinking she was someone else. She put a hand on his shoulder and shook him gently. "Turner, it's me, Lacy."

The scream of a horse rang out in the night.

Lacy pushed harder against Turner. "Something's wrong with one of the horses."

He rolled away from her as if he'd been scalded. "What the hell?" He was trembling as he got to his feet. "What are you doing on the floor?"

The cry of the horse came again, and then the sound of hooves pounding the rocky ground. Lacy jumped to her feet and rushed to the cabin window where a golden orange glow caught her attention.

"Turner, the shed's on fire!" she cried. Before the words were out of her mouth, Turner McLeod was out the door and running as hard as he could toward the flames.

Chapter Five

The flames had caught hold of the old dried wood, and Turner knew trying to stop the fire would be futile. Hell, he'd seen enough fires to know. The only element that nature had thrown on his side was the dampness of the ramshackle structure. The light snow had worked in his favor. Though the ground had not been thoroughly covered, the melt had moistened the most combustible material. With the passing of the storm, the wind had also subsided.

He dashed into the burning structure and brought out the saddles and tack and as much grain as he could carry before the heat drove him out for good.

There was nothing else to do but stand and watch the hay burn.

The horses had managed to knock down the split railing of the corral and were gone. Buster would run with the other horse for a while, but would soon return. Lacy's horse, though, could go anywhere. It was a discouraging thought.

He sensed her standing behind him and knew that when he turned to face her, he would see the one thing he couldn't bear—the suspicion that somehow he was responsible for the fire. But he had a few questions for her, too. Like what had she been doing on the floor with him? And how much of the shed fire and her sudden appearance near Finnegan's Point was coincidence?

He felt her touch on his shoulder. "Turner, are you okay?"

It wasn't the question he expected, and he did finally turn to look at her. He was momentarily dazzled by the way her long blond hair captured the horrible beauty of the flames. He wanted to reach out and touch it, to feel the cool strands of silk that looked as if they were on fire.

"I got the saddles," he answered more gruffly than he'd intended. There had been worry and compassion in her eyes, and that was the very last thing he'd ever thought to see. No, he'd expected a more calculating look as she evaluated the fire and what a great headline it would make.

"The horses?" Lacy looked past him to the corral. "They got away safely?"

"I'm pretty sure."

"The old man at the store said M&M would go back there. Do you think Mr. Weeks will catch him and keep him safe until I can get down?"

Turner was further surprised. Most people would have been concerned only that their convenient transportation was gone. Lacy seemed to care what happened to the horse.

"Melton Weeks seems pretty sharp. And the way that horse is marked is distinctive. Weeks'll know who he belongs to." Both of those things were true. What Turner didn't tell her was that the dangers—for the horse—between the cabin and the store were great. There were wild animals. And no Rex to warn them off on the rugged trails where a horse could slip, stumble or step in a hole.

"As soon as it's daylight, can we start after him and Buster?" she asked.

"Of course." At least she was bright enough to know they couldn't do anything until they had some light. And still, not a single question about the fire.

"All of your hay burned," Lacy noted.

"That's going to be the hardest thing to replace." He and Buster expended quite a bit of effort to get the bales into the shed for the winter. Now he had no hay and no shelter. It was looking as though he might have to relocate a little closer to civilization—a thought that was not pleasing.

"Maybe the forestry people could drop some from a helicopter, you know, like they do for the cows when the winters are too harsh."

Turner looked at her in surprise. He'd become so completely self-reliant that he'd never thought of such a thing. If not the forestry service, perhaps a private contractor. He had the money; he just hadn't thought of it.

"Thanks, Lacy. I'll check into that."

"You'll have to build another shelter."

"Another good point. But we'll see. There's a lot of deadfall around here. It's not that difficult to replace a windbreak and create dry storage for the hay and grain."

"I'm sorry, Turner," she said. "Somehow I feel responsible. Do you think that man who attacked me did this?"

The question was so startling that Turner was speechless. Instead of jumping to the conclusion that *he* was the source of the fire, Lacy had taken the burden of guilt herself—all because of his earlier comment.

He took her arm and gently led her back to the cabin. "No, I do not think the fire was started by the man who attacked you. Before you arrived, someone was outside the cabin. Sometimes hikers pass through, that kind of thing, so I didn't pursue it. But I don't think this has anything to do with you, Lacy. This is about me." He didn't need to tell her that her attacker and his watcher could be one and the same.

When they were both inside the cabin, he knew they wouldn't sleep. They were both worried about what had happened… What could happen. He lit the lanterns and put the water on for coffee. When he looked at Lacy, he saw that she was shivering. It had been a very strange night, and one that still had plenty of unanswered questions.

He'd been in the middle of his nightmare when he'd been awakened by…Lacy. What had she been doing on the floor with him, kissing him so passionately?

"Turner, I've been wondering…why did that man attack me?" she asked. "He could have followed me up here."

He could see she was still worrying. "I don't know why he attacked you. Maybe he wanted your horse, and the horse got away from him."

"It was the strangest thing. He looked like he hated me. He'd never seen me before, and he absolutely hated me. He hurt me without blinking an eye."

Turner listened to Lacy talk and heard the undercurrent of shock. In many ways she was an innocent. She still found it hard to believe that another person could cause pain simply because it gave them power—or pleasure. Yet she was in a business that lived off other people's pain. She was a curious dichotomy.

"Some people don't have to have a reason to want to hurt someone else," he said. He held her cup of coffee and after a moment reached for the bottle of liquor Melton Weeks had given him. They could both use something to warm them up. Lacy was still shivering, and every time she stopped talking, her teeth chattered.

Without comment, she watched him pour a good measure of the whiskey into her coffee cup. When she took the cup from him, she wrapped both hands around it and sipped.

"Now that's got a kick to it," she said, smiling.

Turner couldn't help but smile back. Whatever else she might be, she was a woman with spirit. Plenty of it. She'd been attacked, injured and involved in a fire—and she hadn't whined or complained.

He sipped his own coffee. Melton Weeks hadn't lied—the whiskey was smooth and yet carried a good punch. "I normally don't drink," he said, which was true. He'd given up alcohol when he was accused of starting the second fire. It had been only a garage, but he'd been drinking then, and he'd wondered if somehow he *had* been responsible—some mental force that he hadn't been able to control because of the alcohol. Ever since that time, he'd maintained rigid control of his thoughts, his actions, even his emotions. Except for Lilith.

He put the cup of coffee on the table. "There's something I have to ask," he said. She knew where he was going. A flush crept up her cheeks and yet she held his gaze. Once again a rush of admiration tingled through him.

"You want to know what I was doing on the floor with you," she stated.

He nodded, fascinated by her directness.

"You were having a nightmare. I called out to you, but you didn't hear me. You were very upset, and you were thrashing around." She took a deep breath. "I went to wake you up. Then you grabbed me and you kissed me..."

And she'd kissed him back. He well remembered the feel of her lips, the hunger of her kiss. It was obvious that she was as surprised as he was.

"I don't know what to say, except to apologize," he said. He didn't doubt that everything had happened just as she'd said. Lately he'd been troubled by the recurring nightmare of Lilith's death. He remembered he'd been dreaming, had been fighting the feeling of being tied to the old tree. Living alone, though, he hadn't been aware that he'd actually acted out part of the dream.

"No apologies are necessary," Lacy said. "You didn't know what you were doing. We both got caught by surprise."

He couldn't help but smile. She was generous and kindhearted in sharing the blame and holding no grudges.

"I have a question, Turner. One that you may not want to answer, but I have to ask."

He tensed instantly. "Ask it. As you said, I may not answer."

She nodded. "When I touched you, you were burning hot. It was as if you had a fever. Has that ever happened before?"

The news startled him, but not enough to keep him from realizing where she was going with this. He was hot—and a fire had started. Was there a connection? This was exactly the kind of angle *Texas Legends* would love to exploit. "I don't know," he said, and it was the truth. "Normally I don't have a woman touching me in my sleep." His implication was deliberate and unmistakable.

He saw her eyes widen and knew he'd scored another direct hit. She hadn't expected that verbal assault. He'd as much as said she'd tried to seduce him—the attack was effective.

"I think I'd better try to sleep," she said, turning her back to him as she stretched out on the bed.

There was nothing else for it. Turner blew out the lanterns and took his place on the floor, even though he knew he wouldn't catch a wink of sleep.

LACY DIDN'T MOVE. She pretended to be asleep while she thought of terrible things to say to the man who could change his personality so fast that she never knew what to expect. He'd been friendly and kind— and then accused her of being some kind of tramp. There was something wrong with Turner McLeod— she just wasn't sure what it was. Could be an old-fashioned case of pure damn meanness.

By tomorrow he'd be part of her past. He could think whatever he wanted about her, because she'd be gone and he would be the very last thing on her mind.

She stewed for several more minutes and then found that she was once again thinking about the sequence of events that had led to the kiss.

She'd been innocent of ulterior motives. She'd

gone to him to wake him—to keep him from whatever torments he suffered. And then he'd grabbed her and kissed her and...she'd kissed him back. That was the part that made her squirm with embarrassment. She could have stopped the kiss and she hadn't. She'd given herself to it with heated passion.

She didn't know Turner. Had no reason to trust him or believe a word he said. In truth she had every reason to doubt him. He'd been labeled a fire starter, a man who may have killed his former fiancée—and she'd been rolling around on the floor kissing him like a teenage bimbo.

At the mental picture she had of Erin Brown hearing the details of this latest encounter, she felt her face flush with shame. What was wrong with her, anyway? She'd long ago taken a vow to avoid the complications of a man in her life. Was it because Turner was so obviously unsuited to her that she'd let her defenses down?

She'd been half-asleep. She hadn't initiated the encounter, and at first she had tried to push him away. It was just...she'd been so affected by the kiss. She'd conceded he was a good-looking man, but that had never been grounds for kissing in the past. Her motives were a jumble.

She flopped onto her other side, trying to find a position that would soothe her mind. It would soon be morning, and it was going to be a long long walk down to the store. She needed to sleep, but she couldn't.

Turner shifted on the floor, and she had to fight to keep her thoughts off him. What kind of dream was it that had set him to thrashing so? Lilith was the woman he'd been engaged to marry, the one who had died in a fire. In his nightmare, Turner had been calling out to Lilith, telling her to come out, to save herself.

Whether Turner McLeod was a fire starter or not, he'd certainly had tragedy follow his footsteps. First his younger brother had died in a fire, an accident that had torn his family apart. His parents had died in the past few years, worn down by grief and illness, and then his former fiancée. It was abundantly clear to Lacy that Turner had cared greatly for Lilith. Still did, in fact.

Lacy shifted again and was relieved to see the first indication of dawn. At last the night would be over and she could be on her way.

To what?

It didn't matter as long as it was out of the cabin and away from Turner.

As soon as there was enough light in the cabin to say it was dawn, Lacy swung her feet to the floor. Turner, too, got up, not even pretending to be asleep.

He avoided looking at her, busying himself putting on coffee and the remainder of the biscuits from last night's supper.

"Before we leave I want to check around the shed area," he said.

"I'll help." Lacy took the cup of coffee he offered her, slipped on her jacket and stuffed a biscuit into her pocket. She wasn't hungry yet, but she would be. It was going to be another long day.

They went out together, and Lacy took care to stay behind Turner. She didn't want to mess up any tracks or clues as to who had set the fire. And set it had been. She was sure of it. She was just as certain that Turner hadn't started it—at least, not physically. He'd been with her the entire time. The fact that his body had been so fevered still troubled her, but it was a question she knew better than to pursue. What did it matter, anyway? She was headed home as soon as possible.

She watched Turner as he carefully examined the ground. When he found a muddy track, he let out an exclamation. Lacy bent to examine his finding and realized she couldn't really tell what she was looking at.

"A man of medium weight. Not a heavy man, but not a small man, either. I'd say tall and lanky," Turner said, examining the print carefully.

As she examined the track, she could see the imprint of a waffled sole. Someone else had been near. "Sounds like a description of the man who attacked me," she said.

"Maybe," Turner admitted. "I wouldn't borrow trouble, though. It's a moot issue, anyway. Soon you'll be on your way back to Dallas."

"Thank goodness," Lacy mumbled just loud enough for Turner to hear.

"The track proves that someone was here last night," he said. "Look, there's another." He moved away from her and pointed to another, clearer track.

"I still don't understand why someone would burn down a shed with horses right beside it. They could have been killed." She wondered if Turner might offer some information. If he didn't think it was the same man who attacked her, then who was it? Had he made such violent enemies in his life?

"I suppose we'll know the answer to that when and if we find the culprits," Turner answered. "I wouldn't count on it, though."

She stepped back and away from him when she noticed the huge paw print on the ground. She'd seen enough of Rex's prints to know this was bigger than the dog's. She leaned closer, feeling an unexplained tingle of excitement.

"Turner, what's this?"

He came to look at her discovery, and even three feet from him she felt his body tense. He quickly began to look around the area.

"What is it?" she asked again.

"Looks like a big mountain lion. Some folks around here call them panthers."

"As in black panther?" Lacy knew it was a leading question.

"Same family, but the ones around here are most often tawny." He looked at her, the excitement plain in his face. "Or white."

"Ah, yes, the mythical white panther."

His eyebrows lifted in surprise. "You know the legend?"

"Even down around Merryville everyone's heard of the white panther. Or I should say everyone with a grandmother. It was an old tale. The cat was supposed to roam all over Texas, and since you're the myth buster... I did some research on you."

Turner knelt down by the print again. "Tell me what you know about the cat."

Lacy hesitated. She wanted only to get on her way. Turner's conduct had been less than friendly, and she wasn't in the mood to swap stories with him.

"I'd like to get going," she said.

He glanced up at her. "Yes, I can see where you would."

She saw what might have been regret in his eyes,

but then it was gone. "In fact, I'm ready now. Maybe M&M is somewhere on the trail."

"When we get to the store, I'm going to call the local law officers and report the fire. They may want to question you."

"Great," Lacy said with some heat. "Now I'll have to hang around to clear you of starting the fire. I guess I can just tell them that you couldn't have done it because you were wrestling with me on the floor."

She turned abruptly and went back to the cabin. In her opinion, Turner McLeod was exactly like tar baby. She'd touched him and now it was going to be hell to get away.

TURNER PUT TOGETHER some lunch without saying a word. He'd have to spend the night at the supply store, but his research could wait another day or so.

He would inform the law about the fire. The blame would be put at his door as usual. But it would be worse if he didn't report it and someone else did. Then he would surely be blamed, and Lacy wouldn't be around to confirm his story.

"Let's head down the trail," he said. "We can make the store by early evening, but it's going to be a long hard hike. I hope you're in shape."

"I won't slow you down." Lacy had on her jacket, gloves and hat. "Can I carry something?"

He shook his head. She'd do good to get herself down. He didn't intend to burden her with anything else. "Let's do it."

They started away from the cabin with Rex at their side. Turner cast surreptitious glances at Lacy and saw that she found the hiking exhilarating—for the first hour. When he suggested a rest, she was more than glad to sit. She even took the water he offered, though he could see that it stung her pride.

"I thought we'd find Buster by now," he said by way of conversation.

"What about M&M?"

"Buster knows where he lives, so he'd return to the Point. Your horse knows where he lives, too, and it isn't here." He couldn't help but worry a little about Buster. The animal had uncommonly good sense, but it was a dangerous place.

"Do you still want to know about the panther?"

Turner was surprised. "Sure, it would be a big help to me."

"I'll trade you some information."

He saw that she wasn't kidding. "Okay, but nothing personal."

"You tell me why you're looking for this panther, and I'll tell you my grandmother's story."

It wasn't the deal he'd expected. He'd been certain she was going to ask personal things. But he loved talking about his work, especially about the myths and legends that were the basis for his research.

"The white panther is an old legend that most likely springs from Native American sources. It is a totem animal of great power. The legend says that anyone who see it—and lives to tell about it—will find happiness."

"And you're seeking happiness," Lacy said sarcastically.

"Everyone is. Happiness or death."

He'd unsettled her, which was his intention.

"I know you research myths. I read that in the

background material the magazine sent me about you. My question is, why? Why do you do this?"

Turner thought for a while before he spoke. "There's not a single answer to that question. I've always been fascinated by legends. People want to believe in magic, in miracles, in things that are bigger and better than they are. Wild-creature myths are the most interesting to me. Consider the myth of the unicorn."

"To be seen only by a virgin," Lacy said.

"One of the few legends to give magical powers to a woman, especially an innocent woman."

"I suspect the innocent part was the most important, and it sounds just like something a man would make up."

To his surprise Turner found himself laughing out loud. Lacy was opinionated—and smart.

"The white panther is politically correct," he said, still chuckling. "Anyone can see it and anyone can derive happiness. I personally think it was an image that often came to Indian warriors on vision quests. After a time of fasting and absolute concentration on a spiritual quest, I think the panther vision came to them. The happiness was a result of the hard work they did to achieve a level of self-understanding."

Lacy nodded. "I can see that. So why are you looking for this creature you don't really believe in?"

"Who's to say that a myth can't actually come to life? Besides, two young boys who were lost out here last summer said they saw the cat."

"And did they find happiness?" Lacy asked.

"They were returned to their families, unharmed."

"That's not exactly happiness," Lacy said.

"If you want to do a story for your magazine,

maybe you should hunt down those boys and see if they are happy now. See if their lives were changed for the better.''

Lacy stood up. ''That's not a bad idea. Assuming we ever get back to the supply store and I ever get out of here.''

''What about your grandmother's story?'' Turner asked.

Lacy's smile was only slightly self-satisfied. ''I guess that'll have to wait until the next rest stop.''

Chapter Six

By the time Turner called a halt for lunch, Lacy wasn't sure she had the energy to eat, much less tell a story. She couldn't help but wonder if he wasn't pushing extra hard—just to make a point to her.

She sat down on a rock and unlaced her boots. Her feet felt as if they were on fire. She caught Turner grinning, and she was tempted to throw her boot at him. He, of course, looked as if he'd just been on a leisurely stroll. The man had incredible stamina.

"So what did your grandmother have to say about the white panther?" Turner asked.

Lacy had to bite her tongue to keep from giving him a wiseacre answer. Instead, she forced a sweet smile. "Grandma was something of a storyteller. She said that my aunt Belle saw the panther once when she was a young woman."

She had Turner, hook, line and sinker.

"So what happened to your aunt Belle?" he asked, sitting down on a fallen log so that he faced her.

"She had a very interesting life. Actually, she was my great-aunt. She was born back in the twenties." Lacy would torment him awhile with general facts. "She was the youngest of a large family."

"And what happened when she saw the panther?" Turner pressed.

"Aunt Belle, or Great-aunt Belle if you're a stickler for facts, was a dreamer. She wanted to be a writer, too. But back then children had to work, and Belle's job was to take care of the horses and the cows. Her days were long and hard, from what Grandma Alice told me. Belle was a hard worker, and she had a fondness for the animals. She cleaned out the barn every day and made sure the livestock had fresh hay and water. She was a real stickler for detail, a lot like—"

"You," Turner supplied. "Did the panther follow her into the barn?"

"Actually, no. The barn really doesn't have anything to do with the story. I just wanted to give you an idea of Belle and how her life was. That way you can understand her choices." Lacy hadn't enjoyed herself so much since she'd agreed to take the magazine assignment. For the first time since she'd set foot on this adventure, she had the upper hand.

"Lacy, do you always tell your stories in such a roundabout way?"

"Not normally, but as someone who explores myths and legends, I thought you'd want the entire fabric of the story. I understand that things taken out of context can often be misconstrued."

Her arrow hit home and she saw him wince. He shook his head and stood up. "Okay, I get your point."

"Aunt Belle was out looking for a calf one night. One of the milk cows had calved and neither came in. One of the boys found the mama cow and roped her, but there was no sign of the baby. Belle couldn't stand it. She went out during a storm to find the lost calf.''

Lacy found that now she'd started the story, she really wanted to tell it. Although it was just family legend, it was a story she'd begged her grandmother to tell again and again.

''Belle found the calf. It had gotten tangled in some fence. She cut it loose, but the calf was too weak to walk, so she picked it up to carry it. She wasn't a big girl—tall, but very slender. Still, she picked up that calf and started home.

''She was about halfway when she sensed someone behind her. One of the Oswald brothers had tried to pay court to Belle, but she had refused him. He was a good-looking man, from all accounts, but he had a mean streak. He trapped animals, and he wasn't punctual about checking his traps. Belle said the animals suffered, and he laughed at her. That was it. Belle wasn't much of one for giving second chances.''

''Sort of like you,'' Turner interjected.

Lacy ignored him. ''She knew if she left the calf, he would likely kill it out of meanness, so she wasn't about to put it down and run. She decided to turn around and confront him. Sure enough, it was Roth Oswald, and he'd been drinking.''

''I hope she had a gun,'' Turner said.

''She didn't. But she had nerve. She told him to get lost, and he told her he intended to have his way with her. Then when everyone in the county knew she was damaged goods, she'd have to marry him.

''He was just about to make good on his promise when that white panther came out from behind a rock. The creature sprang on Roth Oswald, ignoring my great-aunt and the injured calf. It knocked him down and tore one side of his handsome face into ribbons, and then it ran off.''

Lacy pulled her boots back on and tied them. "So that's what happened. We'd better get moving.''

Turner reached out and touched her arm. "What about happiness?''

"For Belle? Well, best of all she didn't have to marry Oswald.'' Lacy could contain herself no longer. "And the next week she met a man from San Francisco. A newspaper publisher. He offered her a job that paid a stupendous salary, and the next year he married her. She was able to send enough money home so that her family could hire some help. It worked out for everyone.''

Turner smiled. "It's a good story, but financial security and a job don't make for happiness.''

"They never had children, but they didn't spend a night apart for the rest of their lives. When he died, she didn't last a week after him. Her final words were that she couldn't bear to be parted from him any longer. I'd say she was pretty damn happy.''

TURNER PONDERED the story that Lacy had told, wondering if she'd made it up. She was, after all, a writer. A tabloid writer. Or even worse, a wannabe tabloid writer.

He picked up the tracks of the horses, glad to see they were still traveling together and headed down to the supply store. Still, he was surprised that Buster hadn't come home.

Rex was tracking along with him, seemingly content, and Turner let his mind wander. His gaze lingered on Lacy, in her new boots and tight jeans. She was a sight. She was holding up a lot better than he'd anticipated, and he had to admit that he was beginning to admire her tenacity and courage.

When he saw her begin to limp, he called for another rest break and settled down on a big rock to take a breather.

"How much farther?" she asked.

"A ways." He didn't want to discourage her with actual distances. "I was hoping we'd come across one of the horses."

The words were barely out of his mouth when Rex started whining. He angled away from where Turner was sitting and headed into the brush.

At the sound of something large thrashing in the underbrush, Turner jumped to his feet and took a stance in front of Lacy. Once again he regretted not having a weapon. When he got down to the supply store, he'd heed Melton Weeks's warning and buy a gun.

Turner let go a sigh of relief when Buster's handsome bay head poked out from behind a tree. He greeted Turner with a loud neigh and trotted over.

"Is M&M with him?" Lacy asked, hope in her voice.

Turner shook his head. "I don't see him. He may be close by, but I'd say Buster decided he was getting too far from base camp and stopped. As Mr. Weeks said, M&M would want to go down. That's the way he knows to go home."

"I hope he's not hurt." Lacy walked over and stroked Buster's nose.

"The good news is that you don't have to walk anymore." Turner patted his knee. "Just step up and jump on."

"There's no saddle," Lacy pointed out. "Or bridle."

"He's gentle as a lamb." He could see her hesitation as she eyed Buster's sleek back.

"I don't know."

"Either you ride him or I do," Turner said. "It's a long way down and I'm trying to save you some shoe leather. But if you're going to be as hardheaded—"

"Okay." Lacy put her booted foot on his thigh and swung a leg over the horse's back. "I may be hardheaded, but I'm not stupid."

With Lacy mounted, Turner knew he could pick up the pace. Still tracking M&M, he turned south and started off at a brisk walk. Buster followed, with Rex on his heels.

LACY SAW THE RED ROOF of the store just when she was beginning to think she'd slide off the horse and die on the ground. Her feet were blistered and throbbing from walking in new boots, and now her bottom was sore and aching from the long hours on Buster's back. She was grateful for the ride, but she'd discovered muscles she never knew she had.

"The store!" she said with undisguised joy, and when she heard Turner's amused chuckle, she didn't even have the energy to hurl an ugly remark.

"Delivered safely back to civilization," he said, looking over his shoulder at her with a critical eye. "And only a little the worse for wear."

Lacy didn't even care that he was making fun of her. She wanted to get off Buster's back, get in her Suburban and drive to a motel with a big bathtub—

one with a Jacuzzi. There was a chance she'd done permanent damage to her thighs and butt.

To her absolute relief, M&M was in the corral behind the store, and her truck and trailer were parked exactly where she'd left them. Melton Weeks came out on the porch of the store just as they approached as if he had some kind of radar.

"I thought I'd see you before nightfall," he said, looking past them to the sky. "And you just made it."

"Ms. Wade had a little difficulty," Turner said, not bothering to hide his delight. "She's decided to head home."

Melton Weeks grinned at Lacy. "It's tough terrain for even the most experienced. Don't let him get your goat."

"If I had a goat, he could have it," Lacy said with as much dignity as she could muster. She swung a leg over Buster and slid to the ground with a yelp of pain. Her legs were ruined.

Turner's strong hand caught her under the elbow and held her upright until she could get her muscles to stop quivering and respond. It was just another thing she could hold against him.

"Thanks," she said, shrugging his hand away, aware that though his touch had been only supportive, it had also been warm and comforting.

"I see M&M made it down okay," she said.

"Showed up about four hours ago," Melton said. "He was in good shape and without tack, so I figured he somehow gave you the slip. Didn't think it was an accident, so I didn't get all steamed up about it and call a search party."

"Good thinking," Lacy said, grateful she'd been

spared the humiliation of a search party looking for her.

"So the two of you come on in. I made some fresh coffee." Melton looked up at the sky, then back at Lacy's face. "Whew, girl, looks like you ran into a tree."

"Something like that," Lacy said. She didn't want to go into the details. All she wanted was to get in her vehicle and drive away. She could file a police report from Dallas, for all the good it would do. She'd never clearly seen her attacker.

Melton nodded slowly. "You won't be goin' back to the Point tonight, I don't think. You can stay in the storeroom. Seein' as how the two of you are already chummy, you won't mind sharin' the cot, I don't suppose." He chuckled as he turned and walked back into the store.

"I'm headed for the nearest motel," Lacy said loudly enough for Turner to hear her. "You're welcome to the storeroom, and I know how much you revere your solitude, so you can have it."

"Sure those legs can press a gas pedal?" he asked with a wicked glint in his eyes.

Lacy wanted to do something outrageous, but she simply couldn't manage even a good foot-stomping hissy fit. She was done in.

Turner took Buster and gave him a good rubdown, then turned him out into the corral while Lacy busied herself getting ready to leave. She was about to load M&M into the trailer when she remembered the saddle and gear she'd left behind at Turner's cabin. If it had been hers, she would have sucked up the loss and gone on, but she'd rented the equipment. There was nothing for it but to ask Turner if he would bring it

with him the next time he came down. Melton Weeks
would have to ship it back to the stables for her. She
sighed with frustration. It seemed she was never going
to get free of Turner.

She went back in the store to make arrangements
with Melton. Once her predicament was explained, he
nodded sagely. "It was a pretty nice saddle. Worth
about five hundred, probably. And the gear was
rented, too. I see." He got the stub of a pencil and
scratched on the back of one of his recycled paper
sacks. "That's about seven hundred in gear, I figure.
Yeah, I'd ship it back. Most likely, though, that rental
place is going to want you to pay for it—until it ar-
rives."

Lacy bit her bottom lip. Hell's bells! She didn't
have seven hundred dollars. She was in debt to the
magazine, and now it was going to be more.

"And it'll be about fifty dollars to ship it," Melton
said, still scratching on the sack. "I'll have to have
the cash up front. I'm sure you can understand. You'll
be leavin', and how do I know if you'll ever send the
money?" He laughed. "I know that old sayin', 'the
check's in the mail.'" He laughed again.

Lacy felt in her pocket. She had a few hundred left
from the money she'd taken against the advance. She
pulled off two twenties and a ten and handed them to
Melton. "I would have sent a check. I always pay my
bills."

She hadn't noticed Turner come in behind her or
the look of admiration in his eyes. By the time she
did notice him, she saw only the sardonic expression
she knew only too well.

"I'm off, then," she said, shaking Melton's hand.
"You'll arrange it with Mr. McLeod?"

"Sure," the old man said with a teasing smile. "You two are actin' like you had some kind of lovers' spat."

"Not in this lifetime," Lacy said on top of Turner's quick denial.

The old clerk looked from Turner to Lacy. "There's another old sayin' about protestin' too much. But it ain't none of my business. I'll help you load the horse. If you're headin' out of here, you'd best get goin'. The weather report says there's another chance of snow flurries, and it could get iffy pullin' a trailer down some of these inclines."

Lacy nodded her agreement. *Iffy* was a word she didn't like. She left the store without a word of goodbye to Turner or even a farewell look. He was a bad episode in her life, and one she had no wish to have a parting memory of.

Melton led M&M into the trailer, then she put the key in the ignition, ready to go. When she turned the key, the vehicle didn't respond with so much as a sputter. "Good grief," she said, recognizing the symptoms of a dead battery. She wasn't any kind of mechanic, but if there was a type of car trouble that could be had, she'd experienced it.

With a sinking heart, she got out and slammed the door.

"Tough luck," Melton said, obviously not believing it was tough at all. "Looks like you and Turner McLeod are destined to spend at least one more night together. Maybe you can work out your differences. I mean, a blind hog could see that the two of you are wild about each other."

"What?" Lacy said, offended. "He's rude and difficult and downright nasty."

''And there's somethin' about him that is just like a big ol' jolt of electricity, right?''

''He is shocking,'' Lacy said with as much sarcasm as she'd ever delivered.

''I can tell,'' Melton said gleefully. ''And he feels the same about you.''

''He despises me,'' Lacy said.

''Exactly. But every time your back is turned, he's watching every move you make. He can't take his eyes off you.''

''That's because he doesn't trust me,'' Lacy said. ''Not even as far as he can throw me.''

TURNER WATCHED the entire episode from the window of the store, and he had to admit that he wondered if Lacy had staged the dead-battery incident just so she could stay on and try again for her story. He'd known a few so-called reporters who would do anything for something to write.

He made sure he had his supplies selected and on the counter when Lacy and Melton came back in. If she was staying in the store for the night, he would stay outside. He couldn't head home yet—he had to talk to the local sheriff about what had happened. Of course, it would be a lot better if Lacy confirmed his story, but he'd rather eat grubs than ask her to hang around to talk to the law. Now that she was stuck, though, maybe he could get the local law to come and take a statement from her.

''Looks like the little lady is here for the night,'' Melton said as he stepped behind the counter. He rang up and bagged Turner's purchases without comment. ''Will that be it?'' he asked.

''I'd like to take a look at a gun,'' Turner said with

some measure of discomfort. He'd never been a man to carry a firearm. He knew the uses of one, but he preferred to walk away from a fight with man or animal. But he also knew that he wanted to protect the creatures within his care. Burning down the shed— with Buster and M&M right beside it—could have resulted in the horses' death. That was where Turner drew the line.

"Rifle or pistol?" Melton asked with barely concealed curiosity. He glanced at Lacy again, and Turner was reminded of the bruises on her face.

"Pistol. Someone attacked Ms. Wade on the trail. A tall dark-haired man with brown eyes, camouflage dress, something of an accent. He deliberately hurt her." He hesitated. "And someone burned my shed last night."

Melton whistled long and low. "Burned your shed? Now that's an act of war. Did you get your hay out?"

Turner shook his head. "Some of the grain, but none of the hay."

"Now that's a killin' offense," Melton said without a hint of humor. "Burnin' a man's winter supplies is serious business." He looked from one to the other. "She's attacked on the way up to visit you, and then the shed's burned. Any idea what's goin' on?"

The question caught Turner off guard. He'd developed a theory or two, and not all of them involved Lacy. Someone had been watching him before she found him. Then again, maybe that someone had been waiting for her.

"No," Turner said. "Could be that someone else had plans to use the cabin for the winter. Maybe they think I'm squatting."

"Conversation would be a more reasonable way to

handle it,'' Melton said. "Fire's a deadly thing. Even with that little bit of snow last night, it coulda gotten out of hand and burned half the wilderness. And Ms. Wade's attacker, you'd better report all this to the sheriff.''

"I intend to,'' Turner said.

Melton searched around under the counter and brought out several pistols. "Automatics are faster, but revolvers are more reliable. That's just personal opinion, but it's a common one.''

Turner picked up a small .38-caliber revolver. The gun felt balanced in his hand. He knew enough about guns to know it was more than adequate for how he intended to use it. "This one's fine.''

Melton nodded and added it to Turner's other purchases, along with a box of bullets. After he took the money, he slammed the register shut. "It's dark outside and I'm headed for the house. I'll send my boy over with some supper for the two of you.''

"Please don't bother,'' Lacy interjected. She absolutely didn't want to share another meal with Turner. "We've been enough trouble.''

"Nonsense. The wife's the best cook in Texas. I believe it's ham and sweet-potato casserole and all the fixin's.''

Turner put a restraining hand on Lacy's arm before she could say another word. "Supper sounds wonderful,'' he said firmly. "It's been a long time since I've had a home-cooked meal.''

"Now you two play nice,'' Melton said with a wicked smile. "Funny how feelin's get all scrambled up between folks.'' He was chuckling when he left them.

Turner sighed. He was alone with Lacy once more.

''To put your mind at ease, I'll camp outside.'' He saw the surprise on her face and her quick attempt to cover it. ''I want to check out your vehicle, do you mind?''

She handed him the keys without comment.

Carrying his supplies, Turner went outside, opened the Suburban door and then the hood. Using his flashlight, he shone the beam over the engine. The problem was easy enough to see. One of the battery cables was almost completely missing. Someone had deliberately sabotaged Lacy's vehicle.

Chapter Seven

When Lacy saw the way Turner slammed down the hood of the vehicle, she realized that something was amiss. She closed her eyes, knowing that soon enough she'd learn what it was—and hear how she was somehow behind it all. One thing she'd learned about Turner was that he was paranoid. The man thought every event in the world was some subversive scheme directed at foiling or hurting him.

She heard his footsteps on the porch of the store and mentally prepared herself for another verbal jousting match. She felt her body grow warm and her skin shivery at the thought of him. The man was surely an aggravation.

When he came inside, she stood her ground and waited.

"Your battery isn't dead," he said.

She felt a rush of hope. "Excellent! It's dark, but I can still get to a motel."

He shook his head. "You're not going anywhere tonight. The battery isn't dead, but you're missing a cable. No cable, no juice."

"That's not possible. It drove fine up here." She knew enough to know that if a battery cable had fallen

off her vehicle, she would have been stranded somewhere along the road.

"Yes, it did. So that means one thing. Someone
took the cable while you were gone."

It took all of three seconds for the implication of
that to sink in. "Why? Who would do that?"

"Two good questions. Now how about giving me
some answers."

There was anger in Turner's voice, and Lacy's reaction was a rush of her own temper. "I don't have
enemies, Turner McLeod. I ran a business in Merryville, where I was respected. I got an education and
I got this job. I haven't hurt anyone or done anything.
Maybe before you go pointing the finger of blame at
me, you ought to take a look in the mirror. I'm not
the one folks are saying is a fire starter."

TURNER FELT AS IF he'd been slapped. He knew what
people said about him—wrote about him. But he'd
rarely had someone say it to his face. Lacy's normally
pale complexion was red with anger, and for a split
second he thought he saw remorse in her eyes. It was
gone before he could be certain, and she coldly turned
her back on him.

"I've made arrangements with Mr. Weeks to ship
my saddle and equipment to me. I'll pay you whatever your fee is to bring it down to him at your ear-
liest convenience," she said.

He heard the tremor in her voice and wondered if
it was due to fury or...what? The urge to apologize
to her swept over him, and he started to, but he
couldn't. He simply couldn't. She was what she was,
and he was what he was. An apology might bridge
this moment—which he knew was his fault—but it

would ultimately do no good. There could never be anything between them but the lightning flash of enmity.

The rush of emotion he felt whenever he looked at her was simply the challenge of a worthy adversary, and Lacy was indeed an opponent of merit. No matter that she was willowy and graceful, and that her skin looked as if the lightest touch would leave a bruise. For all her delicate appearance, she had a tensile strength that came from character.

It was a characteristic he admired.

"I'm going for a walk," he said gruffly. He got no reply from Lacy as he banged out the door, Rex at his heels.

LACY STOOD in the empty store and let the chill air cool her heated skin. She was angry and embarrassed. She'd let her temper get control of her tongue, and the result was that she'd hurled the ugliest term she knew at Turner. It didn't matter that her accusation was one he'd heard before. Fire starter. She might as well have called him a murderer. Of all the things she'd expected to see, the hurt that flashed in his eyes was not at the top of her list. In fact, she would have been willing to bet her last ten bucks that Turner McLeod was a man impervious to the slings and arrows of words.

And she would have been wrong.

She found herself listening for the sound of his boots on the porch, for his hand on the doorknob of the store. She would apologize. There was no evidence to show that Turner was a fire starter. She would step up to him and apologize for her rash words and unfair accusation.

Of course, he owed her an apology, too. He'd all but said she'd sabotaged her own vehicle in an attempt to stay another night with him. At the idea, she felt her skin heat up again. The ego of the man! As if she'd do something deceitful just to be around him. After the night they'd spent together, he should know better than that. They were like oil and water. They couldn't agree on anything.

Even as she thought it, she remembered his touch in the darkness of the night. It had been like no other touch she'd ever experienced. His hand on her skin had been magic. Her body had wanted to turn toward him, to feel his arms holding her. She'd denied it at the time, but in the silence of the old store, she faced the truth.

She was attracted to him, which only proved that she was following her mother's tradition of liking the wrong man. If her mother hadn't been out with some tall dark stranger she'd just met, she wouldn't have been in the wreck. And Lacy and her brother and sister wouldn't have been orphaned.

Lacy had a sharply focused mental picture of Turner in her mind. With his lean hips and broad shoulders and air of a loner, he was exactly the kind of man her mother would enjoy. Yet another good reason for Lacy to keep him at arm's length.

Along with getting an education, the other thing she'd vowed was that she wouldn't end up like her mother. No man was ever going to interfere—not even for a millisecond—in her chosen destiny.

The sound of boots on the porch made her heart jump, and she felt keen disappointment when the door opened and a teenage boy came in bearing a tray filled with food. It took only seconds for the delicious odor to reach Lacy, and she realized she was starving.

She helped the boy, who said his name was John. "Thanks," she said, delighted by his open smile and easy handshake.

"Daddy said you had some car trouble. Maybe we can recharge your battery."

"A cable is missing. Mr. McLeod looked under the hood."

John's brow furrowed. "How did that happen?"

"A good question. Ask your father if he saw anyone snooping around the vehicle."

"I sure will, and we'll check the horse trailer before you leave. The good news is that Mr. Otts over at the service station more than likely has a spare cable. That's a lot easier to come by than a battery around here."

Lacy smiled her thanks. When he was gone, she looked at the food. Steam curled off it in the cold store. Turner still wasn't back. She went to the front door and looked out on the empty street. There was no sign of him, and the food was getting cold. She wanted to wait for him as a courtesy. Then again, why? They had no relationship, only animosity. She was acting like an idiot, letting the food chill while she held out some pretense of a friendship.

She was still standing, torn, when the door swung open and Turner stepped into the store. He looked at her, then at the food, and a strange expression crossed his face.

"I think the food's getting cold," he said in an even voice.

Lacy took a plate and sat at the card table by the potbellied stove. A checkerboard was on the table, and she pushed it aside to make room for the food. The last bit of coal was burning down, but it was enough to warm her leg beside the old stove.

"Looks like this might be the social corner of Crossroads," Turner said, nodding at the checkerboard.

Lacy glanced at him suspiciously. He was trying to make conversation. She was instantly alert. Turner was angry with her, and if he was pretending to be otherwise, it was because he had a trick up his sleeve.

"I don't expect sociability will rub off on either one of us," she said. "We don't like each other and we don't trust each other. That's clear enough for me." The apology she'd thought up rose to her lips, but stubbornness made her hold it in check. "You think I'm a conniving reporter and—"

"You think I'm a fire starter who killed my ex-fiancée because she dared to turn me down."

Lacy's fork clattered to her plate. "I don't believe that." She spoke without thinking. "I came up to do a story, but not because I believed you started fires, either kinetically or with a match. My intent in coming up to interview you was to give you a chance to tell your side. In all the articles I read about you, not once did anyone give you a chance to tell your version."

"I had chances. I just chose not to talk."

The arrogance in that statement made Lacy push back her chair and stand up. "You're a fool, Turner McLeod. I assumed you had been tried and convicted by writers who didn't want to spoil a good story by giving you a chance to talk. But if you're too dumb to tell your side, then that's another matter. I can see why people might dislike you."

Instead of making Turner angry, she was shocked to see that he was looking at her with what appeared to be consideration.

"You're saying that my problems are my fault."

"Some of them," she said. "I didn't draw your name out of a hat and decide that I'd make you a media star for a day. It happened. Whether you start the fires or not, wherever you go, fire follows. Look at last night. Look at the shed. If I wanted to go home and make a story out of that, I could—and a damn good adventure tale, too." Lacy was surprised, because she hadn't even considered such a thing. Now she knew that it wasn't a bad idea for a story.

"And I'm sure that's exactly what you'll do," Turner said with some heat.

"I don't know," Lacy answered honestly. "I just thought of it."

"I didn't start that fire."

"I believe you," Lacy said. "I was there. But in the past, there have been questions. Legitimate questions. I only came up here to do a story so that you could have your say. Look at it this way—what could it hurt?"

"I don't owe anyone an explanation when I know I haven't done anything wrong."

"Oh, excuse me. Let me get the Pope so he can make you a martyr. Maybe if you suffer enough, you can make sainthood."

She saw Turner's jaw tighten and knew that her sarcasm stung deeply. She took a certain satisfaction, especially when she looked down and her sweet potato casserole was stone cold. "The food is cold," she said, grabbing her napkin and sitting back down. "I'm eating and then I'm going to sleep. In the morning I'm going to be out of here so fast I won't even leave a memory.''

Turner tossed his napkin onto his lap and began to eat, too. They consumed the entire meal in silence, never once looking at each other.

When he was finished, Turner stood and began stacking the dishes on the tray. ''I'll take this back to Melton, and then I'll find myself a place to camp.''

''Don't be a fool,'' Lacy snapped. ''Stay in the store. We made it one night at your cabin, we can survive another night here.'' It was impossible, but he was trying to heap more guilt on her by making her feel that he was sleeping out in the cold because of her.

''I don't think so,'' Turner said, hefting the tray. ''I'll see about getting your vehicle started in the morning.''

''Consider what I said about the story,'' Lacy said. ''This is your opportunity. As much as I find you to be ornery and hardheaded, I'm not convinced that you're the kind of man who would burn things down. For any reason. This is your chance to have a say, a fair say. If you don't take it, you've got no one to blame but yourself.''

TURNER LEFT THE TRAY of dishes on the front porch of the Weeks home. The lights were off in the house and he didn't bother to knock. Some folks were getting a good night's rest, which was more than he'd get, sleeping out in the cold.

He looked back at the store. It would be a simple matter to go back inside and throw a pallet on the floor. Lacy could have the storeroom with the cot. He wouldn't even be near her. But he preferred the clean outside air to the arguments and accusations that seemed to erupt every time he was near the woman.

In his stubbornness he hadn't even bothered to put together a bedroll, a fact that made him groan with frustration. Then he remembered Lacy's Suburban. It was plenty big enough to sleep in—and probably almost as warm as the store. The idea of sleeping in her ride made him grin, and he even whistled softly under his breath as he went to the vehicle. He pushed aside the supplies he'd stashed there earlier and climbed inside with Rex. Together they'd generate enough body heat to stay warm.

As tired as he was, he fell asleep almost instantly, one arm thrown over the big shepherd. It seemed as if he'd just shut his eyes when he felt Rex struggle beside him and whine. Half-awake, he stroked the dog's head.

"Easy, fella," he whispered. "Let's get some sleep." He felt himself falling back into the black void.

Rex pushed with his nose, and when that got no response, he dug his paws into Turner's side.

Feeling the strong claws rake his ribs, Turner came instantly awake. "Rex," he said crisply, "stop it." For a split second he didn't know where he was. The leather interior of the car seat was unfamiliar, and he felt cramped as he slowly raised himself.

He saw the flames instantly, and the acrid smell of the fire came to his nostrils in the same second. The store was on fire!

And Lacy was inside!

He threw open the car door and raced to the front of the store. Flames had engulfed the door, but he reached through them to discover it was locked. A padlock had been secured on the outside hasp. Someone had deliberately locked Lacy inside the store before they torched it!

The heat of the flames was growing more and more intense with every passing second, and beyond the roar of the fire, he could hear Lacy screaming for help.

He rushed to the back of the store, but there was no exit. The only other option was the window by the cash register. Turner ran there, picking up an old limb on the way. Using all his strength, he heaved the limb through the window. An orange lick of flame jumped into the night.

"Lacy!" he called. "Lacy!"

"Help me!"

He heard her pleas for help and knew she was terrified. Without further thought, he got a running start and dove through the shattered window. He hit the floor in a roll, protecting his head as best he could from the shards of glass that fell with him. The fire was so intense that he thought he'd surely landed in the middle of it.

"Turner!" He heard Lacy's cry of disbelief.

"The window is the only way out," he said, blinking against the heat and the smoke. He coughed, finally catching sight of her pressed against the back wall. "Come on." He grabbed her hand and started to drag her across the store.

Above them a huge timber groaned, dropping an inch. Turner looked up and saw the big support beam hanging on by only a prayer. He pulled Lacy hard just as it cracked and began to fall. Showers of sparks fell in her hair, and Turner beat them out with his hands as she leaned against him, sobbing.

"The window," he said to her again, urging her to keep moving. "It's our only chance." And it wasn't a good one. The open window had given the fire fresh oxygen, just the fuel it needed to burn more fiercely. But they had no choice except to try. If they stayed where they were, they would certainly burn to death.

Lacy was choking and coughing, and Turner put his arm around her, sheltering her as much as possible as he propelled her through the wall of flames and toward the window.

"Jump!" he ordered when they were only a few feet from the window. He did his best to lift and hurl Lacy through the opening. She arched her body and dived, like a diver headed into the final lap of a race. She cleared the window with plenty of room to spare, and Turner gathered his last remaining strength for his own jump.

It was pointless to worry about landing, he thought as he dived through the window into the night. He landed on the ground with a thud and found himself rolling in the cold dirt to extinguish the flames on his shirt where a spark had caught him. When at last he got to his knees, he saw Lacy lying facedown in the dirt.

His heart threatened to stop as he went to her and gently pulled her into his arms. "Lacy, are you okay?" he asked. She was breathing. She had a strong pulse, he could feel it in her throat.

"My God," she whispered. "I was asleep and when I smelled something and opened my eyes, the whole place was in flames." She coughed and sobbed again. "I almost burned to death," she said as if she couldn't believe it.

"You're okay," he whispered, holding her as he

turned back to see the flames spread to all sides of the building.

"Hey! The store! The store's on fire!" He heard Melton's excited voice yelling in the night. "Those people are still inside!"

"We're over here!" Turner called out. "Lacy and I both escaped," he said as Melton and his wife and John rushed over to them. He saw the horror on the faces of the Weeks family as they watched the store that had been their livelihood burn to the ground.

"What are we going to do?" Mrs. Weeks whispered to no one in particular. "Our entire savings were in that store," she said. "We don't have insurance. Can't get it up here without payin' an arm and a leg. Insurance companies won't go for a business here because there's no fire department. Only volunteers."

"Nothin' to be done now," Melton said. "The place is gone."

Mrs. Weeks turned to confront Turner. Her slender body shook with anger. "Melton believes the best of everybody who shows up, and he doesn't have a clue who you are, mister, but I do. I know your reputation. You're gonna pay for this one. You can't go around burnin' people out and get away with it. This one you're gonna pay for if it's the last thing you do."

Chapter Eight

Lacy waited in the small green room with several women, who looked like worried mothers or wives, and a couple of younger men, who looked tough.

A uniformed officer came to the doorway. "Ms. Wade, they're releasing Mr. McLeod now. Step this way."

Lacy followed the female deputy down a hallway and into the Brisco County sheriff's office, where Turner sat in a chair, his back to her. She didn't have to see his face to know he was furious. He'd been arrested and charged with arson before he could even explain. His jeans and shirt were still covered with soot and blood. Probably his blood, from his tumble through the window. He was dirty and he smelled like the fire.

"Mr. McLeod, Ms. Wade has made your bail. You're free to go. Don't leave the county."

He stood up and finally looked at Lacy, but there was no recognition in his eyes. He walked right past her out the door and into the wan afternoon light of the street.

Lacy went after him, more worried than angry. He was clearly traumatized. She wondered if he'd been injured while rescuing her. He'd burst through the window as if he'd been shot from a cannon.

"Turner!" she called to him, and he stopped until she caught up with him. Side by side they continued down the street. It was a medium-size town with the courthouse square and all the little shops around it. Pleasant enough, Lacy thought, if one wasn't being arrested.

"So this is Claytonville," he said. "County seat."

"Are you okay?" she asked.

"Never been better. I never let a little thing like an arson charge get between me and having a good time."

She grabbed his arm and felt the sudden jolt of sensation that happened whenever they touched. "Stop it, Turner. Stop treating me like the enemy. I'm the one who paid your bond, and I'm the one who didn't call the media. I could have sold this story to any news station or newspaper around."

He did stop and turned to look at her. "Why didn't you?"

"I didn't want to, first of all, and..." She knew this was really going to light his fuse. "I paid for your bond with money from *Texas Legends*. I didn't have any other money."

He closed his eyes for a second and sighed. "How much?"

"Five grand. I had to call the magazine and tell them that you'd promised me an exclusive and that you wouldn't run. They wired the money this morning."

"I'm not telling you a—"

"—damn thing," she finished for him. "I know that. I didn't really expect you to, but I didn't have any money, and no one in Crossroads was willing to help you out. Heck, they were all ready to lynch you.''

''I know.''

''It was call the magazine or leave you in jail. I can promise you, another hour or two and the national media would have been all over this.''

''I'm not giving anyone an interview.''

Lacy had expected this. She shrugged. ''I think you're a fool, but it really is your decision. All I ask is that you pay the magazine back in full. I won't have a job there, so it's not for me. I just feel they should be paid back, and I think it's your place to do it.''

Turner looked at her. ''Fair enough.''

She stopped in front of the Suburban she'd rented. The horse trailer wasn't hitched to it.

''Where's M&M?'' he asked.

''I took him and Buster to a ranch outside of Pecos. The owner is watching them, and Rex is with them. I'll take you there and then back up to the supply store, or what's left of it. You can get back to your cabin from there.''

Turner climbed in the passenger seat of the truck. ''Why are you doing this?'' he asked.

She got behind the wheel and started the engine. ''John found a cable for me and put it on.''

''Answer me, Lacy. Why are you doing this?''

She held the steering wheel but didn't put the vehicle in gear. ''I don't know,'' she said, finally looking over at him. ''You saved my life. You came through that window and saved me. Why would you do that if you meant for me to die in the fire?''

"The front door had been padlocked. Someone deliberately set that fire. With you inside."

"I know. A gas can was found behind the store. The last I heard, there were no fingerprints on it."

"I didn't set that fire."

"I happen to believe you." She was looking deeply in his crystal-blue eyes. "Do you think someone was actually trying to kill me?" she asked. This was a question that had hounded her all night.

Turner didn't answer immediately. She saw that he was really thinking the question through. "I don't know," he said. "Were you the target, or were you the intended victim to make it not just an arson charge against me, but a murder charge? Did they think I was in the store with you, and you were just an innocent bystander? I wish I knew the answer to even one of those questions."

Lacy had considered them, too. And she had no answers.

"Turner, if you aren't responsible for the fires, why are these things happening?"

He swung around to face her with anger in his eyes and the corners of his mouth, but then his face softened. "I can't keep getting angry when people accuse me of these fires. It's more than coincidence. Something *is* happening."

"What?" She put it to him as bluntly as possible.

"I don't know."

She believed he was sincere. The thought that somehow Turner was involved in the fires and wasn't even aware of it crossed her mind. "These last two fires, you were outside not long before the fires started, both times."

"What are you saying?" he asked harshly.

She reached across the seat and touched his arm, surprised yet again by her reaction to the contact. She kept her fingers lightly on his arm. "Is it possible that somehow you do things you don't remember?"

"You mean like pour gasoline on the store, padlock the door so you'll burn to death and then light the fire?"

Lacy held his gaze. She wasn't going to back down now that she'd asked. There were cases where people went into a kind of blank limbo-land where an alter ego took over. Dr. Jekyll and Mr. Hyde came to mind.

"I did not start those fires. Not in a blackout state or fully conscious."

"How can you be so sure?"

"Because my own brother burned to death. So did Lilith. I know what it feels like to lose someone by fire. I wouldn't do that, not even in some kind of fugue state."

"Would you be willing to undergo some testing?"

"As in what kind of testing?"

"I don't know. A lie-detector test." That was the only thing she could think of.

"Lacy, if I were setting the fires in a subconscious state, then I'd pass a lie-detector test with flying colors."

"Then how can we prove you're innocent?"

"I guess I'll have to hire a baby-sitter. Someone can watch me day and night, and then when the next fire starts, I can prove I didn't have anything to do with it."

Lacy looked straight at him. "I'll do it on the condition that you give me an interview. Once we prove you're innocent, you have to give me the story. An exclusive."

Turner took a deep breath. "I've never seen anyone more determined. Is the story that important to you?"

"You couldn't begin to imagine how important it is. I simply can't go back to the magazine and say I failed."

"Okay," he said. "I'll give you the interview. I'll tell you everything."

Lacy heaved a sigh of relief. Turner had finally seen the light. He finally understood that she wanted a story that told the truth, not one that simply made a splashy headline. And she was going to get it—her first published article.

TURNER REGRETTED HIS OFFER as soon as he made it. But he couldn't withdraw it. He saw how important it was to Lacy. And she had paid his bond—with money from her magazine.

She also seemed willing to believe he was innocent. Or at least, willing to entertain the possibility.

She'd accurately pointed out that in both the last fires, he'd had opportunity to set the blaze. That was the problem. In all the fires, he'd had opportunity and means, and what some thought passed for motive. The only reason he hadn't been formally charged before now was there had been no physical evidence.

There was no physical evidence in this case, but the weight of his reputation had been enough to get Brisco County Sheriff Paul Taylor to file a charge. It was a long way from a conviction, but it was one more step toward disaster for Turner.

He watched as Lacy maneuvered the Suburban into traffic. Out of the corner of his eye he saw a television van. WRRK from Dallas was on the scene. He'd gotten out of jail in the nick of time.

"Don't take me to the supply store," he said, realizing that other news media would probably be there waiting.

"Where to?" Lacy asked.

He didn't know. "Buster and Rex are okay?"

"Fine for the moment. Rex was whining and missing you, but I assured him you were going to be fine."

Turner felt a wave of gratitude toward Lacy. Even when the chips were down, she'd been the one to look after the creatures that were his friends and companions.

"Thanks, Lacy. It seems I owe you a lot more than an interview."

He could see his words touched her by the way her hands tightened on the steering wheel and her jaw tensed a little.

"I owe you an apology," he said, amazed at how easily the words came out. "I accused you of things that weren't true, and I didn't give you a chance. If you'd treated me the same way, I'd still be sitting in a jail cell and you'd have a sensational headline for your story."

Lacy kept her hands on the wheel and her eyes on the road as she drove them out of town.

"For what it's worth, Turner, I don't think you're a fire starter. I don't know what's going on, but I don't believe it's you. I hope to goodness it isn't." She finally glanced over at him, and the innocence in her eyes made him want to protect her. "If you are some kind of fire demon, I'm in a world of trouble."

He could resist no longer. He reached across the seat and put his hand lightly on her head. His fingers slid through the silky blond hair. "Your trust means more to me than I can tell you." His chuckle was bitter. "You're the only person who'll even give me a chance. Fancy that, and you work for *Texas Legends*."

"Where do you want to go?" Lacy asked.

He could see she was at a loss for what to do with him. He didn't know himself. He didn't want to go back to Crossroads, though. "There's another way up to the cabin. It's a bit longer, but it's not that bad. I'd like to continue my research while I'm still a free man. Of course, that means you'd have to come with me." He watched her expression carefully and almost smiled when he saw how excited she was.

"I want to know all about your research. I think that's an important part of the story."

"I would hope so," he said, meaning to tease her. She was so sincere, though, that she didn't even know he was pulling her chain.

"Yes. I think that if people understand what you're doing, they'll have a much better appreciation for the kind of man you are."

"You mean as defined by my job?" He was teasing again, and once more Lacy let it go right over her head.

"That's exactly right. I mean you're a man who searches out myths and legends. That's not an ordinary job. It takes a lot of dedication and determination."

"What if I just want to see the white panther so I can find happiness?"

She gave him a long look. "I know you're pulling my leg. I'm not dumb. I just chose to ignore you. But if you do see that white panther and it does change things for you, I guess you won't care what I write, because you'll be so blissful that my journalistic endeavors won't even touch you.''

Turner laughed out loud, and he found it a strange and pleasant sensation. How long had it been since he'd actually given in to a big full laugh? He didn't know the answer to that question.

''I'm glad I entertain you,'' Lacy said, but she chuckled, too.

''I think we got off on the wrong foot before. This time I'll make sure that we have an amiable relationship,'' Turner promised. ''It's the least I can do.''

''This assignment might not be half-bad,'' Lacy agreed. ''I think you're making the best decision.''

''I think I'm making the only one open to me,'' Turner said with a smile to take away the sting. ''Let's go get Buster, M&M and Rex, and head up to the cabin. I'll tell you all about my work on the ride there.''

''I think the sheriff is going to be annoyed with you,'' Lacy said. ''It's going to take a county employee two days to let you know about your court date, but we're going to tell him where we're going.'' She pulled out the cell phone, which was useless in the wilderness, and made the call.

''Thanks,'' Turner said. ''Keep me on the straight and narrow.''

Lacy's face grew troubled. ''What about supplies?''

Turner gestured toward the back. ''I put all the stuff in here before the fire. I was angry and I intended to set off for the cabin at dawn. I didn't want to go back into the store, so I slept in here with the supplies. What I bought will last us for several weeks.''

"We don't have saddles," Lacy reminded him.

"No better way to learn to ride than bareback. You can ride and I'll use Buster as a packhorse to carry supplies. We can rig something up. The horses will do fine on grain, but I'll need more hay before winter sets in."

"Okay," Lacy said dubiously.

"Remember, you're the one who made the bargain," Turner teased her, and found that he took great delight in it.

"I'm not complaining. I'm just dreading," Lacy said.

He put a hand on her shoulder and felt instant desire for her. What had he gotten himself into? He quickly removed his hand and settled for a verbal compliment. "You aren't a complainer, Lacy. You've got a lot of grit."

"Well, thank you kindly, sir," Lacy said with a thick drawl.

"We'll have to camp tonight and then set out early tomorrow. It's going to be a long day."

"So what else is new?" Lacy quipped.

THE NIGHT WAS COLD, but the Suburban blocked the wind, and Turner and the dog provided some small amount of heat. Lacy had determined to keep her distance, but as the hours of the night ticked on, she found herself pressed against Turner with the dog on the other side of her.

Sandwiched between a German shepherd and a man charged with trying to kill her by starting a fire. It had turned into some kind of adventure.

The trouble with her current situation was her own imagination. Turner's hand had drifted over her ribs, resting with his thumb occasionally brushing her breast. He was asleep—and she intended to leave him that way. But she was awake, and very much aware of his touch.

She was nuts. That's all there was to it. And she would have only her own craziness to keep her company until dawn, which could not come soon enough.

At the first streak of light, she felt Turner stir, and she moved away from him. Her body was stiff and sore, and she wondered if she had enough left of the grit Turner admired to get back up on a horse and head into the wilderness.

Turner gave her no time to think. As soon as he was up, he began preparing the pack. When they'd picked up the horses, they'd bought some grain from the rancher. They had everything they needed—at least for a while.

It was barely light when Turner lifted her onto M&M and he led the way with Buster. Lacy snuggled as deeply as possible into her coat and tried to focus on the wild beauty of the landscape.

"It's going to be a long hike," he said over his shoulder, never breaking his stride. "We'll keep a steady pace as long as possible. If you get too tired, just tell me and we'll rest."

By lunchtime, Lacy was so sore and weary that she almost slid off M&M's back. Turner caught her, his strong arms breaking her fall and setting her on her feet. She saw the worry in his eyes.

"I'm okay. Really," she insisted, embarrassed by her lack of stamina.

Instead of letting her go, his arms tightened around her. Her gaze connected with his, and Lacy felt as if time had stopped. When he lowered his lips to hers, she met him halfway, eager for the kiss.

He was both tender and demanding, and Lacy moved into his embrace. She needed his strength. Her own emotions left her knees trembling even as she wanted more.

The pale winter sunlight sparkled on the needles of the spruce trees, leaving Lacy with the feeling that she'd stepped from the world she knew into an enchanted land. Her arms circled his neck, her fingers finding purchase in his thick hair.

Somewhere there was the loud cry of a bird, and the sun moved behind a cloud. Lacy felt Turner's hand on her back, urging her even closer. Her own body craved the deeper contact.

It wasn't until Turner's body stiffened and he broke the kiss that she heard the soft growl of the dog by her side. She looked down at Rex, who stood ready to attack. Another low growl issued from deep in his chest.

Turner pressed her down by a boulder.

"Stay here," he said.

"What is it?" Her heart hammered.

"I don't know."

Lacy scanned the distance but saw nothing. She looked back at Turner. He was tensed for action, like the dog. Both were totally focused on the treeline a dozen yards away. Lacy couldn't stop the return of the memory of the man who'd savagely attacked her. Turner had never filed the report on the shed fire, and she'd failed to report the attack. So much had happened in Claytonville, and freeing Turner had been her only goal. Now she regretted her oversight.

Easing away from her, Turner moved to Buster and

reached into the makeshift pack. When his hand came out, he held the revolver he'd purchased from Melton Weeks.

"Turner!" she whispered. The sight of the gun was terrifying.

"Be quiet," he said softly. "Be quiet and stay behind this rock. I'm going to find whatever's out there." He finally looked at her. "Lacy, if anyone or anything comes toward you, run into the trees."

"Turner, don't! Just stay here."

"We're sitting ducks if we ride on. There's a perfect place for an ambush about half a mile from here and no way to go around it. This is better ground for a fight if we have to have one."

"You're in enough trouble." She knew that convincing the sheriff—or a jury—that Turner was acting in self-defense would be difficult.

"I can take care of myself," he said, his hand grazing her cheek. "And I'm counting on you to take care of yourself. We're partners, remember?"

She nodded, unable to answer. She was so afraid. She held her breath as she watched him move behind the horses and slip quietly into the trees. With the dense growth for cover, he disappeared in a few seconds. Rex was at his side.

All around her was only the stillness of the wilderness.

Chapter Nine

The midday sun cast stark shadows in the dense undergrowth, and Turner moved very carefully. Rex trotted ahead, and he let the dog guide him. He had no idea if it was man or beast that had gotten Rex so disturbed, but his guess was man. The two horses had not reacted, and they would have if there had been a predator near.

"Easy," he whispered, stroking Rex's back as the big shepherd tensed and crouched, ready to spring. Though Turner scanned the area, he saw nothing except boulders and trees.

A breeze stirred the cedar limbs, and Turner saw the brief flutter of something white. Rex, too, saw it. The dog began to move unerringly toward it.

Turner didn't know what he expected, but the filmy piece of lace tied to a tree branch was the last thing. It was so feminine, so completely out of place, that he halted a good ten feet away for a better examination.

At last he moved toward it and saw the note that was attached. He recognized the handwriting instantly, the slope of the letters, the big capital T that was written with a flourish. It was Lilith's handwriting. Impossible as it might be, the note was from her, and it was addressed to him.

He flipped open the folded note and began to read.

Dear Turner,

It's only my fear that makes me write this. I am terrified, for you and of what will become of you. Last night, when I returned your ring, I tried to explain why I could no longer see you. I know you didn't understand, and I wanted to try once more. Again, though, I find it impossible. My love for you is undiminished, but my fear of you is greater. Please make no effort to contact me. This is for the best, for both of us.

Lilith.

Turner folded the note and reached to untie the lace that had bound it to the tree limb. He recognized that, too. It had been torn from the nightgown he'd given her. Holding the lace and the note, he felt as if the woods around him had suddenly changed. He no longer recognized the ground under his feet or the trees surrounding him. He might as well have been on Mars.

How had the note come to be in the wilderness? Lilith was dead. Dead and buried. It was impossible, and yet he held both the note and the lace in his hands. He looked down at the sheer white material, the diaphanous webbing of the old lace. Lilith had loved the gown. And she had looked a vision in it. But it had been destroyed in the fire, along with his dreams and hopes and the woman he loved.

So where had the note come from?

It was almost as if Lilith was speaking to him from

the grave, telling him that she was afraid of him. Turner finally felt the brutal pain of that accusation. The woman he had loved—had hoped to marry—had died afraid of him and what he might do.

He tucked the note into his jacket and tried to regain his equilibrium. Above him a red hawk circled, crying into the noonday light. Rex sniffed the ground.

Turner fought to regain control of his emotions and forced himself to think.

Lilith was dead. Someone else had left the note.

Systematically he began to search the area. There were two sets of prints, neither of them clear in the rocky ground. All he could tell was that they were distinctly different. Two separate people had been at the site.

The neighing of a horse reminded him of Lacy, and a rush of fear went through him. She was alone. Defenseless. He turned and began to hurry through the trees to the place he'd left her.

''Turner,'' she said when she saw him, relief evident on her face. ''Did you find anything?''

He started to reach into his coat for the note, then stopped. He didn't suspect her of involvement. Not really. She knew about Lilith. She'd done her research on him. And ever since her appearance, strange things had begun to happen in his life. But she'd been with him, and there was no way she could have known about the alternative route up to the cabin. Not even the most avid hikers used the old forgotten trail. Still, he'd learned that it was better to be safe than sorry.

''Nothing of any importance,'' he said, unable to hide the fact that he was lying.

''Turner?'' Her face was cast in worry. ''What happened?''

He shook his head. "It must have been a bear or something. I didn't find anything. Let's get back on the trail. It's going to be a long afternoon."

Before she could ask any more questions that required a lie, he grasped her waist and lifted her onto M&M. The gelding stood solid as a rock, and Turner picked up Buster's reins. The horses, too, were tired. Turner knew that before night fell, he would drive them all even harder to make the cabin.

LACY TRIED TO RELAX the muscles of her legs and butt and back, but each step the horse took only reminded her that she was sore. Sore and weary—and afraid.

Something had happened to Turner when they'd stopped for lunch. He'd kissed her. And it wasn't a kiss that a woman could easily forget.

Apparently, though, he'd forgotten it. For the past four hours he'd acted as if she was a stranger. Worse than that, as if she was a stranger he didn't like.

She had begun to vacillate between anger and a kind of emotional turmoil that made her question her memory. Without any prompting, Turner McLeod had taken her in his arms and given her a kiss that had scorched itself into her very heart. She had only read about a kiss that could be felt from the toes to the top of the head. Now, she'd experienced that kiss, and Turner was acting as if he couldn't remember her name.

In the past four hours he'd spoken to her exactly twice. Once to tell her to hang on to the horse's mane when they went down a ravine and forded a stream, and the other when he'd told her to get off the horse and take a brief rest.

He'd offered her no help in mounting or dismounting, and he'd walked into the nearby woods and remained there for the entire rest break.

"It's about another five miles to the cabin," he called back to her now.

"Turner, can we stop for a few minutes?" She couldn't go a step farther without talking to him.

"Best if we keep walking," he responded without slacking his pace.

"I want to stop." And she did. She pulled M&M to a halt with the old bridle they'd bought from the rancher in Pecos and slid to the ground, her feet vibrating with the shocking pain of her weight after hours of being numb.

"Lacy," Turner said, not bothering to hide his exasperation. "It's getting dark fast."

"I can see that," she said. "What I can't see is what's eating you?"

"I want to make the cabin before it's dark," he said.

"Why? What's so terrible about the dark?" She saw that her question had pulled him up short.

Turner wouldn't look her in the eye. "It's safer for you in the cabin. I'm tired. The horses are tired. This isn't the best time to be out."

Lacy watched every nuance of his expression. Though he was speaking to her, he didn't meet her gaze. He was acting as if he had something to hide.

"I've spent a lot of time listening to people talk," she said slowly. "Odd how people will tell you the most intimate details of their lives without batting an eye. They'll tell you their salaries, bank accounts, number of lovers, how good their last lover is or was, but then all of a sudden, they'll clam up over the most insignificant little thing. Such as where they got their earrings. It's a very telling thing.''

"Lucky I'm not wearing earrings," Turner said, edging away from her.

"Are you sorry we kissed?" She wasn't going to let him off the hook. All afternoon she'd been in a hellish limbo, wondering if the kiss they'd shared was the cause of his sudden desire for solitude.

His gaze locked with hers. "Yes," he said softly but distinctly. "I'm sorry. It never should have happened." He walked away from her, picked up Buster's reins and headed up the trail. He didn't even turn around to see if she was following.

TURNER CURSED HIMSELF with each step. He might as well have slapped Lacy in the face. He couldn't have hurt her more. This was what he got for breaking his vow to stay away from everyone—women, men, children. They had no place in his life. Whenever he allowed himself to get close to anyone, tragedy followed.

Lacy was just the latest victim, and luckily it was mostly her pride that would suffer. But he was at fault, for allowing his desire those delicious seconds of free rein.

The moment he thought of kissing her, he realized that he wanted to feel her lips beneath his again. The surge of desire for her only added to his frustration and anger. He cast a quick glance behind him and saw her, tired and confused. She was leading her horse, and he knew she was too sore to ride farther. The trip had been grueling for her. It took all his restraint not to walk back to her and explain.

But what could he say? That he'd found a note

from a woman he'd loved, a woman who had died in a fire? A woman who had died afraid of him?

He picked up his pace, wanting only to get back to the cabin. He'd leave Lacy there and head out into the woods to search for the white panther. His only solace was his research, and that was where he intended to put all of his thoughts, energy and emotion.

When at last he saw the cabin in the small clearing, he felt as if a heavy weight had been lifted from his shoulders.

"Thank goodness," Lacy said, halting. "I didn't think we'd ever make it."

"Can you make some coffee?" Turner asked. "I'll unpack and settle the horses."

"Sure," she said, walking past him toward the cabin.

Turner watched her until she went inside. As tired as she was, her spine was ramrod straight. She did have a lot of grit.

He unpacked Buster and gave both horses a measure of grain while he set about repairing the corral fence. The damage wasn't too bad, and after he found some wood and mended the fence, he turned the horses into the enclosure. Before real winter set in, he'd have to figure out a way to build another lean-to for Buster.

Unless he was in jail.

For a few hours he'd been able to put the fire at the supply store behind him. When he was alone, trying to sleep, he knew the fire would come back to him. The horror of the blaze, the dread that Lacy was trapped in the burning building. The burning fever of his own body whenever he dreamed of fire. The dark questions haunted his subconscious. Why was it that everywhere he went, fire followed?

"Turner?"

He looked up to find Lacy standing not ten feet away. "What?"

"I want to talk to you."

He had no doubt that she did. And he was pretty certain he knew about what. "Okay," he said, falling into step beside her as they went into the cabin.

She served him a cup of coffee, and from the aroma he knew it would be good. "No trouble with the stove?" he asked.

She shook her head. "No." Her gaze met his.

"Lacy, I think it would be best if we gave up this whole idea. I've been thinking about it, and this may be dangerous for you. It was selfish of me to ever agree to it."

"I never took you for a coward, Turner," she said.

Her words stung, and his first reaction was to deny them. Instead, he nodded. "If being a coward will keep you from getting hurt, I won't mind the label."

"What happened on the trail?"

She was smart, too. She'd put two and two together, and she wasn't going to quit insisting that she had four. "Nothing that will make a difference to you."

"Try me," she said, eyes unwavering. "Turner, I just ruined the lower half of my body riding bareback for nine hours. I'm not going back down that trail tomorrow. I'm here, and this is where I'm staying."

He wasn't surprised. "Lacy, it's your safety I'm concerned about."

"What happened on the trail?"

He broke eye contact and moved to stand by the

window. Night had already fallen. Through the tree limbs he could see millions of stars.

"I'm going out to hunt the panther," he said, looking for any excuse to leave her in the cabin. "You can stay here." He turned back and thought he caught the glitter of tears in her eyes. But it must have been a trick of the lantern on the table. When she spoke, she was angry.

"If my safety was really a concern, you wouldn't leave me alone. Remember, Turner, our agreement is that I stick to you like glue, twenty-four hours a day. If I'm not with you, you don't have an alibi if a fire starts."

"So far, I haven't been accused of burning forests," he said dryly.

"You're in serious trouble, Turner. Melton Weeks may doubt your guilt, but his wife doesn't. She's the one who called the law on you. And from what I could see of the other members of the Crossroads community, they're only too eager to believe the worst."

"That's human nature, Lacy. Haven't you learned that by now?" Even to him his words sounded bitter.

"So why don't you start by telling me the truth. Start with the first fire, your brother's death."

"I had nothing to do with my brother's death!" Turner's denial came out harsh and angry, and he realized that he was clenching his hands. He forced his fingers to relax and his voice to soften. "I loved Benjamin. His death put my parents in an early grave. I lost everything I cared about."

"And inherited considerable money," Lacy reminded him without batting an eye.

"I see you've read all the other magazine pieces

about me. Yes, I inherited some money. That's a fact. Make what you will of it.''

"How did the fire start?"

He was suddenly weary. "Electrical," he said. "An extension cord behind my bed had been worn in half."

"And you escaped."

He wondered if she'd taken classes in cruelty. "Don't you think that point haunts me? I escaped. I woke up and went to my parents' room and got them. We tried to get to Benjamin, but the fire was too hot by then. The firemen came and made us leave. They said Ben was dead from smoke inhalation."

Lacy's hands were gripping the edge of the small table, but she wasn't finished.

"And Lilith, what happened in that fire?"

"That's not open for discussion." He didn't have it in him to relive it. At night, in his dreams, he revisited the fire. Not as it had actually happened, but as it had become twisted in his mind.

"When you go on trial for setting fire to Weeks Supply, you'd better believe that all this will come up whether you want it to or not."

"I'll deal with it then." He threw some clothes onto the bedroll he'd made on the floor. "I'll be back in the morning. I'll leave Rex to take care of you."

"I'm your alibi, Turner. You need me."

He took a long breath. "That's where you're wrong. I don't need anyone."

SHE WATCHED HIM pick up his things and walk out of the cabin. From the window she could see that he didn't take a horse, and she was relieved.

She could no more have gotten back on a horse

than she could fly, and it was going to be a lot easier to track him on foot. And track him she would. Or follow him. He wasn't going to get far enough ahead of her that she'd need tracking skills. Turner might be someone who reneged on deals, but she wasn't. She intended to keep him in her sights the entire night.

The little voice in her head that she always tried to ignore told her that she was being very stupid. She was unarmed and really unprepared for a night outside. She'd bought her jacket with an eye more toward fashion than warmth. Heck, who needed a coat in Dallas?

As soon as she felt certain Turner wouldn't be expecting her, she snapped a lead rope on Rex's collar and opened the door.

The wind was cutting as she stepped out of the shelter. "Find Turner," she told the dog, who was already striking out on the scent of his master.

Lacy had a good memory of Turner's normal stride. She'd ridden behind him all afternoon. She tried to pace her own steps so that she could stay close, yet far enough away that he wouldn't detect her. Of course, eventually she needed to be able to see him if she was actually going to watch him.

Lucky for her the moon was nearly full, and the silvery light was bright enough to cast shadows. She and Rex caught sight of Turner in the first ten minutes. He was a good distance ahead, moving swiftly. Rex gave a low whine, but Lacy managed to convince the dog to be silent. She'd never seen a dog as smart as Rex, and she was glad for his company.

Turner angled off the trail but never slackened his

pace. Lacy could only imagine that he knew where he was going.

For the first half an hour, the thrill of spying on Turner kept her preoccupied. But the game quickly grew tiring as the cold penetrated her jacket. Her fingers, especially on the hand holding Rex's lead, felt as if they had frozen permanently.

Turner halted and began to examine something at the base of a tree. To her surprise, she heard a loud oath just as something snapped sharply in the night.

Rex whined, and Lacy quieted him again with a pat. The dog was completely focused on Turner, as was she. What had he found?

He started moving again and she was able to get to the spot. The trap there was the biggest she'd ever seen. The jaws were huge. Turner had triggered the release, and the serrated edges were no longer dangerous. Beside the trap a rabbit, used for bait, lay limply. She knew without touching it that it was dead.

When Rex made a move toward the creature, Lacy pulled him back. "If you'd reached into the trap for the rabbit, you'd be dead," she warned the dog. The huge jaws would have closed on Rex's head.

She fully understood Turner's anger. Leghold traps were some of the cruelest devices used by people who called themselves hunters. Mostly the humans who deployed such traps were after the fur of an animal. They didn't want the pelt marked or destroyed, and it didn't matter to them that an animal caught in such a trap suffered horribly.

"The white panther," Lacy said, knowing instinctively that she was right. Someone was out to trap the panther. The white hide would be incredibly valuable.

Goose bumps jumped on her skin, making her even

colder than before. Perhaps this was what Turner had found on the trail that had upset him so. If someone had put out leg traps—not caring who or what stumbled into them—Turner would consider them to be dangerous.

Rex tugged on his lead, and Lacy had to leave the sprung trap behind. Surely Turner would pick it up on his way home.

She let the dog lead her deeper into the woods. Though Turner was out of sight, she had no doubt Rex would follow him. All she had to do was keep walking. And avoid any other hidden traps.

She'd just caught sight of Turner when she heard the loud snap of metal again and saw him stumble. He didn't cry out or indicate in any way that he was hurt—he simply fell.

Rex jerked free of her grip and began to run toward his master, and Lacy forgot her soreness and cold as she raced after the dog. She knew without looking that Turner had been caught in one of the deadly traps.

Chapter Ten

Turner saw the trap just as it snapped shut on his leg. It had been hidden underneath dead leaves and limbs, a perfect trap for an unsuspecting creature, man or beast.

The jaws snapped with such force, Turner thought his ankle might have broken. He tumbled to the ground, his only hope for his leg the stout boots he wore.

For a second he remained prone. The pain was intense, and he waited for the shock that would give him a few moments of numbness. When he sat up, he realized the trap was chained to the base of a tree. Cursing, he grabbed the chain and jerked it. The heavy links weren't about to give.

Turner realized he was in serious trouble. The moonlight was bright enough to reveal the jaws of the trap clamped firmly on his leg. It normally took two people to open the trap and set the release. Injured, with his own leg in it, he probably would not have the strength to free himself.

Trapped and wounded. If there was a predator nearby, he would be a perfect victim—if he didn't freeze to death.

He heard something coming toward him through the woods, and he turned with his back to the tree. Pulling the handgun he'd bought from his jacket, he prepared to fight.

"Rex!" He recognized the dog instantly—and the tall slender woman who was right behind him. "Lacy!" He was so relieved to see them that he didn't bother to get angry.

"Turner, are you hurt?" She unsnapped Rex's lead and knelt down beside him. "My God, your leg!"

The strong jaws of the trap were digging into his muscle, and Turner put the gun down to free his hands. "Maybe together we can open it," he said. He had to stay positive. If he showed fear, Lacy might panic. She was already distressed.

Together they tried to force the trap open. It gave only a fraction and then closed tight again, forcing a groan from Turner.

"Who would do such a thing?" Lacy asked as she tugged at the trap.

"Find a big stick," Turner said, forcing the pain from his voice. "Maybe we can pry it open long enough for me to slip my foot out."

Lacy didn't need to be told twice. She searched the area until she found a stout limb. At Turner's direction, she forced the limb in beside his ankle.

"Get another limb," he said. "Once we pry it open, insert the other one."

It took a little longer, but Lacy found another solid limb and brought it back. Turner talked to her as they used one limb to open the trap and the other as a block.

The progress was slow, millimeter by millimeter, and he could sense Lacy growing tired. She was put-

ting everything she had in the effort. "Just a little
more," he encouraged her. "It's going to be tricky
for me to get my foot out. If I dislodge the limb…"
He didn't have to finish. The trap would snap shut
again, this time on his foot.

"Turner, maybe I should go for help."

"Go where?" he asked. "Even if we had a cell
phone, it wouldn't work out here. We're too remote.
We're on our own, Lacy, but you can do this. I know
you can."

His simple encouragement seemed to be all it took
for her to put one last effort into the job. With a cry
of success, she moved the jaws open another inch—
enough for him to use the second limb as a block.
With great care he eased his foot free.

The loud snap of the jaws let him know he'd made
it just in time.

"Is it broken?" Lacy asked, tossing her limb aside
and bending down by his leg. Her fingers moved carefully from his knee to his ankle.

"I don't know," he said. "You might be the better
judge of that."

"My younger brother was always doing something
foolish. I think he broke every bone in his body at
least once. I thought for sure he'd be the death of me.
He'd come in limping and bloody and off we'd go to
the emergency room. That got expensive, so I started
learning how to tell when his injuries were serious or
not."

As she talked she gently pressed around his ankle.
Turner wanted to yell with pain, but he knew she was
being as careful as she could.

"We should get that boot off," she said. "The

swelling is going to be bad. If I don't take it off now, we'll have to cut it off.''

''I don't know.'' Turner didn't relish the idea at all. They weren't that far from the cabin, about half a mile. But how was he going to get there?

Lacy began unlacing his boot. ''I don't think it's broken. At least, it's not a compound fracture. We need to get the boot off, stabilize the ankle and then elevate it. Tomorrow I can ride down for help if it seems necessary.''

Turner had no argument. If Lacy had not come along, he could easily have died. Like it or not, if his leg was badly injured, he would have to rely on whatever help Lacy could manage to get for him.

He gritted his teeth as she eased the boot from his foot. Although he wasn't looking, he listened intently to her.

''I can't be certain, but I think you may be the luckiest man I know,'' Lacy said. ''It looks bruised but not broken. I'll be able to tell more when I can actually see,'' she added.

Turner gave a half laugh, half groan. ''My confidence in you is undiminished, even if you can't see.''

''I knew you'd feel that way,'' she replied, her hand gently brushing his knee. ''I'm sorry, Turner. I know you must be in a lot of pain.''

''Nothing compared to what it's going to be like when I get up and start to walk.''

Lacy's hand pressed down more firmly on his leg. ''I don't think that's a good idea.''

''Whoever set these traps will be back to check them. Eventually. Somehow I don't think he's a very nice person.''

''He didn't intend to trap a human,'' Lacy said.

"He didn't care," Turner retorted. "The kind of person who does this type of trapping simply doesn't care who or what gets damaged. I don't want you here when he comes back, and I don't want to be here." Turner knew only too well that rather than face the legal consequences of the leghold trap injuring a human, the trapper could decide to take the easy way out—which wouldn't be a good thing for him or Lacy. He had a gun, but there was no guarantee a poacher wouldn't simply shoot them in the back.

Instead of arguing, Lacy looked around the area. "I know you're hardheaded enough to do exactly what you say. So—" she dragged another limb over beside him "—I think we should try to make you some kind of crutch."

Turner wanted to hug her. When the chips were down, she always seemed to come through for him. "Good thinking, Lacy. You know, you have a lot of grit for a tabloid reporter."

He couldn't see her expression with her face tilted down in concentration as she figured out his crutch, but he had no difficulty hearing the sarcasm in her voice when she answered.

"Thanks, I was thinking something similar about you—you sure are accident-prone for a macho wilderness man."

Turner was still chuckling as he took off his belt and began to help Lacy fashion the two limbs together, using the lace of his boot.

It was going to be slow going back to the cabin, but Turner felt a strong compulsion to get back there. As soon as his leg was better, he'd have to thoroughly check the area all around the cabin for more traps.

And then figure out how to set his own trap. He

wanted the person or persons using the leghold traps. If they were the two men who were after the white panther—as he suspected—he had every intention of convincing them to leave Texas and never come back.

LACY HAD FINALLY GOTTEN a grip on the almost paralyzing fear that had overtaken her when she realized Turner had been caught in the leghold trap. Now she had slid emotionally into that automatic pilot that mothers and responsible adults have to learn to cultivate. She'd examined Turner's injuries and come up with the best plan she could think of to make him safe and keep him safe.

As she used every bit of her strength to help him to his feet, she hoped she'd be able to sustain her facade of calm strength for a little longer. She was going to need it to get him back to the cabin.

His understated caution about not wanting to be there when the trap owners returned had chilled her to the bone. The man who'd stepped out and grabbed M&M's reins was still clearly etched in her mind.

He'd been a mean bastard who felt no compunction about hurting her. No telling what he would do to a wounded man.

With each step farther away from the trap, she felt better.

Turner stumbled and only her quick reaction saved him from falling on ground littered with sharp rocks.

"I'm going to owe you big time for this," he said.

"You don't owe me anything. Helping another person isn't a debt service." She believed that, but it also made her feel good that Turner acknowledged she didn't *have* to help him. And not a single word of complaint about her following him. She smiled to herself.

Up ahead, Rex patrolled the barely visible trail, and Lacy took a great deal of comfort in the dog's vigilance. It allowed her to focus completely on helping Turner.

"Why did you follow me?" Turner asked. His words came out short and choppy because of the exertion he was making to move forward.

"I knew it couldn't last," she said lightly. "I was wondering how long you could restrain yourself."

"Believe me, I'm not complaining. If you hadn't come along, I'd be in the trap yet. And I'd probably starve there or freeze."

Unless the trapper came back. Neither of them needed to say those words.

"I made an agreement with you, Turner. You're in serious trouble with the arson charge. I said I'd watch you twenty-four hours a day to prove that you aren't setting fires. When I give my word on something, I do my best to follow through."

She bit her lip when she finished, hoping she didn't sound too prissy. Maybe she should have thrown in the Girl Scout pledge at the end.

To her surprise, Turner laughed. "For a woman with a surprisingly sunny attitude most of the time, you can sure nail a guy's hide to the wall."

"I didn't mean—"

"Maybe you didn't, but it's quite clear that while you're a woman of honor, I'm a scoundrel who reneged on his half of the bargain. I tell you I'm sending you home and I go off into the night, only to nearly kill myself. You follow and then save me. I see a definite moral to this story."

Lacy was glad it was dark and that her hair hung over her cheeks. She didn't want Turner to see her big grin. He'd followed the storyline very clearly. For all his bluster and bossiness, he could see his own errors.

"I don't know that I want to do the interview, but I do owe you an apology. And a debt of gratitude," Turner said. "The irony here is that I haven't apologized to anyone in twenty years, and now I've given you two apologies."

"Apologizing isn't a sign of weakness, Turner."

"I'm not sorry I kissed you."

The words were so unexpected that Lacy stumbled. Turner's hand on her shoulder easily steadied her.

"We're a pair," she said, still confused by his confession. "One's injured and the other's clumsy."

"You're a long way from clumsy." His hand lightly rubbed the taut tendons on her shoulder. "You're a very special woman, Lacy. I realized that before tonight. But I want you to know that I see qualities in you that make me believe there are still good people out there."

Lacy swallowed. "Thanks, Turner." This wasn't the time to tell him that she wanted the public to see the things about him that she saw. That maybe if he let down his barriers a little and simply talked, those who were so ready to condemn him might surprise him.

The feel of his hand on her shoulder changed. While she'd been concentrating on helping him, she'd been able to stifle the pulse of desire that his touch always seemed to awaken in her.

Now, though, his words had triggered her memory of the kiss, and his fingers were moving sensuously over her neck. She couldn't help but wonder if he was deliberately igniting her passion.

If so, this time she wouldn't fall for it. Her reaction to Turner's kiss had badly frightened her. She'd kept her emotions so carefully controlled for so long. Taking care of her siblings, running the beauty salon, getting her education—there had been no room for emotional involvement. She hadn't allowed herself even to want a man's touch.

But Turner had awakened all those dormant feelings, and they had come back with a vengeance.

"We'd better move on," she said.

"We're halfway there," he told her.

"We'll make it," she answered, more to reassure herself than him.

By the time they got back to the cabin, they were both exhausted. Lacy gathered ice from the horses' trough and packed Turner's ankle. In the light of the lantern, she could tell that the bone wasn't broken, but his leg had already begun to swell and turn an ugly purple.

Against his protests, she'd put him in the bed and made him as comfortable as she could. When she offered him a glass of Melton Weeks's liquor, he took it willingly.

It seemed to take the edge off his pain, and she watched as he fell into a fitful sleep. She moved to the bedroll she'd made on the floor and let exhaustion drown her own doubts and misgivings. There was nothing else she could do until morning, anyway.

THE MOSS IN THE OLD OAK TREES swayed sensuously in the soft breeze that seemed to carry the smell of the Gulf of Mexico. He stood beneath the branches of a tree, caught by the bends and crooks that looked so strange and dramatic in the light of the full moon.

Not fifty yards away, the small Creole cottage seemed like a fairy-tale creation. Moonlight gilded the roof a bright silver, and lacy white curtains billowed at the open windows.

He felt the need to hurry to the cottage. Though the night seemed filled with enchantment, he was uneasy.

Then he saw her. She came to the window, dark curls hanging over her shoulders and falling to her breasts. The white nightgown drifted against her body, outlining it. She held something in her hands.

"Lilith." He spoke her name. He loved the way it rolled off his tongue, a name fitted perfectly to the woman.

"Lilith," he said again, this time more loudly.

She saw him then, and he waited for the smile of recognition and delight that always crossed her face.

Instead, her mouth set in hard lines. She held up a hand, palm outward.

"Stay away," she called. "Stay away from me."

He saw the flames then. It was almost as if the moonlight had ignited them. They danced along the glitter of the silvery roof. They were playful flames, darting and teasing on the wind.

Standing at the window, Lilith wasn't aware of them.

He started running toward the cottage.

"Get out! Get out!" he cried. But he had no voice. The sound was only a croak in his throat.

"Stay away!" She held up her hand and there was fear all over her face. "Stay away!" In her hand was a piece of beautiful white lace.

"Lilith, the cottage is on fire," he tried to tell her. All she had to do was climb out the window onto the safety of the dewy grass. He ran harder, realizing that he made no progress. He was exactly where he'd started, beneath the branches of the old tree.

The harder he tried, the more he realized he was bound to the tree. Looking behind him, he saw the chain that held him. It wrapped around his waist and circled the tree. Try as he might, he could not free himself.

When he looked back at the house, it was completely engulfed in flames. Lilith was nowhere to be seen. Instead, standing in the open window was Lacy. Someone stood behind her, holding her as she struggled to free herself. Above her the orange flames gobbled at the roof, growing bigger and hotter with each second.

"Lacy!" he cried.

LACY THOUGHT FOR A MOMENT that she'd been slapped. Something woke her so harshly that she sat straight up. Then she realized Turner was thrashing on the bed. He was mumbling something, but she couldn't understand what he was saying.

Easing to the bedside, she put a cool hand on his forehead. He was feverish, and he was fighting as if a band of demons had infected his sleep.

"Turner," she said softly, "wake up. You're having a bad dream."

She was completely unprepared when his arms circled her and pulled her onto the narrow bed with him. He buried his face in her neck and held her, his breathing harsh and rapid. "It was the same old dream,'' he said, ''except this time it wasn't Lilith in the burning house. It was you.''

''It's okay,'' she soothed. ''It was only a dream. Everything is okay.''

His lips caressed her just below the jaw, a tantalizing touch that grew into a nibble as it moved along her jaw to her ear. His warm breath in her ear sent shivers through her entire body as his hands began to move from her arms to her back, pulling her even more tightly against him.

Wearing only her panties and shirt, Lacy felt his arousal. Subconsciously she'd wanted his touch. When his lips claimed hers, she opened her mouth. She wasn't a passive recipient of his kiss. She captured his tongue, hungrily, eagerly, and heard him groan in response.

His hands slid beneath her shirt and up to her breasts. Her own hands were busy, moving along his ribs, down the lean muscle of his hip.

Somewhere in the back of her mind a small voice warned her to stop, but she paid no heed. She wanted Turner. For all of his thorniness and irascibility, something in him touched her in a way no man ever had.

There's always a price to pay for going after what you want, and Lacy was willing to pay whatever necessary for the feel of his hand sliding over her hip, breezing across the sensitive skin of her stomach and inner thigh, teasing her into near panic as it moved to a more intimate place and then withdrew.

''Turner,'' she whispered.

His response was to lower his lips to her breast.

Lacy felt her back arch and knew the true meaning of sweet torment.

His hands captured her hips, lifting her on top of him. Lacy stopped thinking, stopped trying to make sense of the rush of emotion that overwhelmed her. It was all she could do to hang on to Turner and survive the whirlwind of sensation and pleasure that threatened to turn her inside out.

WHEN THEY'D PLAYED OUT their passion, Lacy found that she was lying on his chest, her damp hair spread over him. She could hear the hammering of his heart and knew that it matched the rhythm of her own.

Comforted by that sound, she felt her body begin to relax. Her hand reached up to brush his face, delighting in the stubble of his beard. There were so many sensations, so many feelings that were new and wonderful to her. How silly she'd been to try to convince herself that she didn't need to be loved.

And she had no doubt that what she felt for Turner was love. Strange as it might seem to anyone else that she'd fallen in love with a man she barely knew—a man charged with one arson and accused of more— she didn't find it odd at all. There was a noble streak in Turner's nature, one that made her believe in him.

She smiled against his chest. She did believe in him. And there had to be a part of him that believed in her. No man could make love as he just had, injured leg and all, unless he had strong feelings for his partner.

"Turner?" she said softly, shifting so that she could cuddle against the length of his body.

"I'm sorry, Lacy," he said in a cool voice.

"Sorry? For what?"

"I was dreaming again. It was the same dream. Lilith was in the house. The fire was all around her, and I couldn't help. And then it was you, not Lilith. You were there, struggling to escape and yet you couldn't. Someone was holding you. And then you were in my arms. You were here with me, so alive and so real. You were safe.'' He hesitated. ''But for how long? How many hours or days before the next fire?''

Lacy's skin felt as if an icy wind had blown over her. ''It was just a dream, Turner. I'm here and I'm fine.''

''And how many regrets will I have for this moment of pleasure?'' he asked.

Chapter Eleven

Turner felt the woman in his arms grow stiff. His hand drifted through her long hair, feeling the silky texture. How could he explain to her that the horror of the dream was more real because of the joy of her company? He'd been so careful not to let anyone close enough to hurt him again.

"In the dream Lilith was so real and so alive. Yet she's dead. Because of me. I didn't start the fire that killed her, but I accept the blame."

He still held Lacy's hair in his fingers, and he slowly twisted it. It was such straight hair, nothing like Lilith's curls.

"I'm not Lilith," Lacy said softly. "You blame yourself for what happened to her, but if you didn't start the fire, you aren't to blame."

He had no answer. The joy he'd shared with Lacy was simply more than he could risk. How could he explain that to Lacy Wade, girl reporter? She was a woman who courageously risked everything for him.

His fingers tightened lightly in her hair, and he wanted to pull her mouth to his for another kiss. He wanted to tell her how much she'd come to mean to him in such a short time. But that would surely be signing her death warrant. Everyone who came close to him got burned.

"Lacy," he whispered into her hair, "this wasn't a good idea. Your being here isn't good. Not for either of us. The past is too much present."

He expected an argument, but Lacy remained still, her breathing shallow and rapid. He could feel the tiny puffs of her breath against his chest.

"Are you okay?" he asked.

"I'm fine," she said, sitting up so abruptly that he felt as if something had been stolen from him.

She found her clothes in the darkness and began to pull them on.

"Where are you going?" He only wanted her to come back to his arms, and yet he couldn't ask it.

"I have to go outside," she answered in a voice so flat it sounded completely emotionless.

"Take Rex with you," he said. He reached out and his hand touched her hip. She jumped away from him as if his touch burned. Then she was out the door with Rex at her heels.

Turner eased himself up in the bed. His ankle, which he'd completely forgotten about in the heat of passion, was now throbbing. He shifted to try to make it more comfortable and to keep an eye on the door for Lacy's return.

His mind drifted back to her kisses, to the feel of her body beneath his hands and mouth, and to her own touch traveling over his skin. He felt another surge of desire for her. She'd won a place in his heart, and though he'd fought it tooth and nail, he could no longer deny that he had feelings for her. He couldn't deny them to himself—or admit them to her.

What he really wanted was to take her back into

his arms and make love to her again so he could watch the expression on her face, see her reaction to his touch. He wanted to learn everything about what pleased her.

How long had it been since he'd allowed himself to feel anything for someone? And Lacy had overwhelmed him with the effect of a sledgehammer to the head. He was smitten by her.

As the minutes dragged by, he began to grow more worried. It didn't take forever to go to the bathroom, especially not on a bitterly cold night.

He shifted up in the pillows. What a fool he could sometimes be. Lacy was upset, and he was the cause of it. His worry was relieved only when Lacy came back into the cabin. She arrived on a burst of cold air and the sound of the door closing, none too gently, behind her.

"I'll be gone first thing in the morning," she said, and her voice sounded odd. In the darkness Turner couldn't see her features. "I'll go down and send some medical help up to you. You'll be happy to know that when I write my story, I can report that you have talents other than those you're accused of."

Turner felt as if he'd been reinjured. Lacy's attitude as much as told him that now that she'd slept with him, she was done. Had it been some kind of ploy on her part, some manipulation to get close to him? For her career? The very idea was infuriating.

"I suppose you got your story, then," he countered, letting his anger rule his tongue.

"Oh, I've got a story," she said. "Just not the one I thought I'd get."

"Is this the tactic you normally employ? If you

can't get an interview legitimately, you crawl into bed with the guy?''

There was a pause before she spoke. ''I haven't developed any tactics. This is my first assignment. But you've given me something to think about.''

Turner wanted to put his hands on her arms and hold her until she came to her senses. The idea that Lacy might end up in another man's bed was absolutely intolerable to him—and that she would use it as a weapon against him only further infuriated him.

''Women!'' he said harshly.

''Not women! Woman! There's only one woman for you, Turner. I'm talking about the woman you loved—still love. Lilith Ascenti. The woman you wanted to make love to tonight. I was just a substitute. And of all the things I thought I might find in this cabin, feeling like a substitute for your dead lover wasn't one of them.''

LACY COULD NO LONGER contain the hurt. The blame didn't all rest on Turner's shoulders. She knew better. She'd known it even as she was succumbing to his touch, his kisses. But knowing that she was equally at fault didn't mitigate her pain.

All the while she'd been allowing herself to feel for Turner, he was imagining she was someone else.

Humiliation made her want to go back outside and stay. Only the cold kept her in the cabin.

''Lacy,'' Turner said softly, ''please light the lantern.''

''Go to hell,'' she said bitterly. Things were bad enough. She wasn't going to let him see her cry.

''We need to talk.''

''I need to get out of here,'' she answered. His

voice sounded worried, as if he cared what she thought or felt.

"Please, light the lantern. Or else I'll get up and do it."

It was a foolish threat, but one he must have known would work with her. Turner shouldn't be on his leg. She wiped the tears from her cheeks, took a deep breath to calm herself and did as he asked.

In the soft lantern glow, she saw that he was worried. He was staring at her.

"What makes you think I wanted you to be Lilith?" he asked gently.

"Don't treat me like a child," she said. "You made love to me and then told me it was a mistake. Because of the past. You've been living like a monk since she died because you still love her."

Turner didn't say anything. "I loved her a lot, but I know she's dead. Sometimes I dream about her. I was dreaming—it's almost always the same dream. She's in the cottage and the flames start on the roof. I try to warn her, to go to her, and I can't. I'm always restrained."

"You were dreaming," Lacy confirmed. "I got up to check on you. I was afraid you'd developed a fever. I touched your face and then…" She couldn't go on. It was too intimate, too humiliating.

"I'm sorry," he said softly. "It seems I spend a good part of my time apologizing to you, but I'm sincere."

"Apologies can't help this," she said, fighting back the tears. "I know you didn't mean to do this. I knew better."

"Would you do something for me?" he asked.

In the lantern light, his eyes were soft, concerned.

Lacy started to say no, but something made her stop. "What?"

"Come over here and sit beside me." He patted the bed.

"Are you crazy?" she asked.

He shook his head. "Not in the normal sense. Crazy with worry about you, maybe."

"Don't bother. I'm sure I'll recover. And I don't think I'll use this as a tactic for getting stories. It's a little too embarrassing and painful."

"That's good to hear," he said. "Please, just come sit on the side of the bed. I want to tell you something."

Lacy almost refused, but to do so would make her look even sillier than she already felt. He was injured, so he couldn't get up and grab her against her will. It was pretty obvious to both of them that he wouldn't have to use force on her, anyway. She'd fallen right into his bed and made love to him without any restraint.

She walked over to the bed and sat on the edge within touching distance of Turner. He was still bare-chested, and the chill in the room made gooseflesh rise on his muscled arms.

"What is it?" she asked, unable to meet his gaze. She was so ashamed!

His finger lifted her chin till she finally met his gaze. "I'm not in love with Lilith anymore. She's been dead for three years now. Three long years. I did love her greatly, but time does help heal losses."

"Turner, you may not think you're in love with her, but you are. I realize now that you were so passionate when you touched me because you wished I was her. A man doesn't touch a woman with such tenderness and passion unless there's emotion there—''

"There is."

"And it isn't just sex." She stopped. "What did you say?"

"I'm falling in love with you, Lacy. I've fought it, but I can't help myself. Against all common sense, my feelings for you are growing stronger and stronger."

Lacy took a deep breath. Even though she was looking directly into his eyes, she couldn't tell if he was playing her like a fiddle. Turner McLeod was a loner, a man who kept to himself. And here he was admitting that he was developing strong feelings for her. More likely he was just trying to make her feel better for acting like such an idiot.

"Nice try, but I'm not buying into it."

"You don't have to believe me," he said. "Maybe you shouldn't. But if you don't run away, maybe I can show you. I was dreaming of Lilith, but then she turned into you. You were in danger. You were going to be hurt, and it was because of me. Lacy, I can't risk losing you. I've lost too much that I love."

"I don't want to be hurt, either," she said, and was surprised at the tears that sprang to her eyes. Turner had tremendous power over her, she couldn't deny it.

"I won't hurt you," he said, his finger brushing her cheek. "The reason I didn't want to let you close to me was not because I'm still in love with Lilith, but because I didn't want you in harm's way."

She felt as if she were falling into his clear gaze. He was so easy to believe, so convincing. Was it possible he was telling the truth?

His hand slipped down to her shoulder and moved

along her arm, igniting small fires of passion at each inch. He lifted her hand and brought it to his mouth, kissing her palm gently.

"Tell me about Lilith," she said simply.

He put her hand down but still held on to it. "Okay." He looked long into her eyes. "Lilith had broken our engagement. I had already left St. Martinsville at her request. I'd spent the night in La-Fayette in a motel, and I was headed for the interstate and Texas when Lilith's brother, Anthony, got behind me in his truck. He was wild. He kept ramming his truck into the back of mine like he wanted to push me off the road and kill me, which is exactly what he intended.

"I stopped and got out, and he came up to me and punched me in the face. It wasn't until after we'd fought and I subdued him that I found out that Lilith was dead. Her cottage had burned, a fire starting in the attic. All her windows were open. She could easily have gotten out and saved herself."

"But she didn't," Lacy supplied.

"No, she didn't. No one knows why. Anthony and her family believe that I hurt her. That I knocked her unconscious and started the fire."

"And the police?"

"They had no physical evidence to tie me to the fire. I also had a receipt from the motel in LaFayette. Unfortunately there was no one in the small bar drinking the night I spent there. No one remembered me, at least."

Lacy paused, then asked, "You were in a bar drinking all night?"

"I was torn up. Lilith's rejection had devastated me. It's difficult for me to care about someone, to allow myself to be vulnerable. It had taken months with Lilith, and we had spun so many dreams about our future together. Her rejection was almost unbearable.''

Lacy admired his honesty, his candor at admitting pain. ''There was no one in the bar?''

''I'm sure there was, but to be honest, by the wee hours of the morning, I couldn't have identified myself. I tied one on. There must have been people in the bar.'' He shrugged. ''People don't ever really look at a drunk. Avoidance is the best tactic.''

''What about the bartender?''

Turner hesitated. ''The bartender said he didn't remember me. I thought that was odd, too. It certainly didn't help matters with Lilith's family. They still hate me and blame me for her death.''

Lacy sighed. ''What a tragedy.''

''Lilith was a remarkable woman. I guess I'll always wonder why she changed her mind. She never said. She just called me on the phone and said that it was over and she didn't want to see me again. She asked me to leave town immediately.''

''And you honored that request?''

Again Turner hesitated. ''No. I went by her cottage once. She was inside, and I didn't quit pounding on the door until she came to it. She was crying and she looked so unhappy. She begged me to leave, and leave quickly. She said she couldn't bear it for me to be there.

''So I left and I never went back. The idea that I'd caused her so much unhappiness when we had both been so filled with plans for a wonderful future...it almost killed me.''

Lacy blinked back her own tears. What could have

gone wrong? A lot of the answers to Turner's troubled past lay in figuring out the answer to that question, she was sure.

"Was anyone ever arrested for the fire?" she asked.

"To my knowledge, no one. As far as I know, it was ruled accidental."

Lacy had an idea. It came to her full-blown and filled with potential.

"Why don't we go back to St. Martinsville and see if we can't figure out what really happened?"

"No!" The word was like an explosion.

"Why not?"

"For a lot of reasons. Her family, for one. It would horrify them to see me again. I don't think you understand the depth of their hatred for me. And St. Martinsville is a small town. Within five minutes of my being there, everyone would know about it."

"Is it that, or is it because you're afraid of what you might uncover?" she pressed. Lacy understood Turner's reluctance to go back, but she was certain that the only way to secure the future was to search the past.

"I don't know what happened with Lilith—why she broke our engagement, why she didn't try to save herself—but I do know that I didn't hurt her. I would never hurt anyone, much less someone I love."

"It's time to quit running, Turner. It's time to turn around and confront what's been happening in your life. I think now is the time you should do it, when you have me by your side."

She saw the consternation shift to hesitation, then to wonder. "You'd go with me?" he asked.

"I would insist. I don't know what's going on, but

all of these fires can't be a coincidence. If you aren't starting them, someone else is. There's a good chance someone killed Lilith in order to pin the blame on you. Isn't it worth a little bit of pain to find out who did that and why?''

"Put that way, you're right. I just can't believe anyone would willingly hurt Lilith. Everyone in town loved her."

"Maybe they didn't mean to kill her. Maybe they only meant to burn her house and blame that on you. But someone is very likely guilty of murder. That someone may have followed you here to Texas. I think it's time you faced him, before someone else is injured or hurt."

"Like you could have been in that store."

"Exactly," Lacy said.

TURNER'S RESISTANCE to what Lacy was saying began to crumble. In the rubble that was left, he discovered that he wasn't shocked at the idea of someone trying to frame him for setting fires.

Deep down, he'd always suspected such a thing, but he'd never allowed himself to explore the idea. It was too awful, and it still made Lilith's death his fault. She had died because someone was trying to get to him.

He wanted to stand up and walk out into the night, but his ankle wouldn't allow such antics. He had to sit and confront his own thoughts. The only redeeming thing was that Lacy was sitting right beside him.

His fingers brushed her skin, gliding over the flawless contours of her face. She gave him such pleasure. Just to look at her was a delight. To touch her was paradise.

"Thank you, Lacy," he said, and drew her closer to him.

She didn't resist, and that fact made him bold enough to kiss her. Although she seemed more tentative, she kissed him back. It took only a few seconds for the passion to flame between them. It was the most delicious blaze Turner had ever felt.

"Come here," he said in an emotion-roughened voice as he pulled her down beside him.

She reached over to turn off the lantern, but he caught her hand. "Leave it on," he said. "I want to look at you, and I want you to have no doubt that I'm making love to the woman I want. The beautiful woman I'm holding in my arms right this moment."

Her tentative smile was one of the best things he'd ever seen. Somehow he'd made her understand that he cared for her, not someone from the past. And he'd begin by showing her, by giving her as much pleasure as she could stand.

Chapter Twelve

Sunlight brightened the interior of the cabin when Lacy finally forced herself out of Turner's arms. The lantern had burned out near dawn, as she and Turner had finally given in to sleep. Sleeping next to him, cradled in his arms, had been one of the best nights of her life, and she had awoke with a sense of purpose.

Outside, the horses frisked around the corral, their hooves striking the hard ground as they bucked and played. Rex slept by the door. Turner, too, remained asleep. She slipped out from beneath the covers and hurried into her clothes. The cabin was cold. She needed to start a fire and make some coffee.

By the time the old stove was going, Turner was watching her, a smile giving his face a youthfulness that she'd never seen on it.

"Good morning," he said.

"Yes, it is, isn't it?" She couldn't stop the smile that reflected her happiness.

"You're mighty spunky in the morning," he said, yawning and stretching, revealing his lean upper torso as the covers slid down.

Lacy enjoyed the view as she heated water for coffee. "I have every reason to feel like a million dollars. And I do."

"I'm feeling pretty good myself," he said, swinging both legs off the side of the bed. "In fact, I'm feeling good enough to get dressed and go outside."

Lacy almost stopped him, but held her tongue. She watched him closely as he pulled his pants on and got to his feet. His ankle was swollen and badly bruised, but it wasn't nearly as damaged as she'd feared it would be.

"We need to check for more traps," he said.

"I can do it." In the daylight she could be very careful.

"I want to cut the chains and collect the traps we already know about." Turner was already lacing on his boots. "I think if I'm careful, I'll be okay."

"I know better than to argue," she said. "We'll gather the traps first."

"And then you're determined that we go to St. Martinsville." He buttoned his shirt and slipped on his jacket.

"It's your call. I know I'm right, though."

"I think you may be."

She was stunned to hear that admission. "Want some breakfast?"

"Grab some biscuits and we'll take a thermos of coffee. The sooner we get going, the better."

"I'll meet you outside."

She quickly prepared the coffee and food and met him in the sun beside the cabin. Turner walked slowly and with care, using the makeshift crutch he'd improved with some whittling and baling twine. Still, the effort to walk taxed him. By the time they got to the first trap, he was ready for coffee and a break.

Sipping the hot coffee in the brisk air and bright sunlight, Lacy couldn't help but admire the woods around them. They could have been a million miles from anyone else in a paradise of natural beauty. Instead, they were pulling up vicious traps. When Turner indicated he was ready to move on, Lacy gathered the thermos and cups and began to search again for the traps.

Turner had warned her to be careful, and she used a stick to probe beneath limbs and leaves in places where a trap might be.

There was a loud snap, and she looked to see Turner freeing his crutch. He'd brought a pair of bolt cutters and quickly snapped the chain. He threw the trap into the middle of the path for them to retrieve later.

"How much territory do you think we need to cover?" Lacy asked.

"There's no way to be sure, but my guess is that the trapper would have an idea that the animal he's after has been near this place. Then he would saturate the area with traps. The other method is to put the traps near watering holes, but that doesn't seem to be the case."

"Should we set up a grid of some kind?" She could see Turner was impressed with her question. "I was the best Easter-egg hunter in Texas when I was a child. I had a system."

They both laughed, shaking off some of the macabre aspects of their chore. Three hours later they'd gathered six traps and were ready to head back. She had just taken Turner's arm when she heard the click of a bullet being injected into a chamber. She swung around to confront a wall of trees.

"Hold it right there."

The voice came from a thicket, and Lacy instinctively froze. Beside her, Turner remained relaxed, but she could tell that he was prepared for action. His hand edged closer to the jacket pocket where he kept his gun.

"You wouldn't be intending to steal my traps, now would you?" the man asked from behind the trees.

"Yes, that's exactly what I'm doing," Turner said evenly. "Do you have a trapping license?"

"It's a free country," the man said, stepping out from the cover, a high-powered rifle pointed at Turner and Lacy.

Lacy heard Turner's sharp intake of breath.

"Anthony, is that you?"

"Indeed it is, Turner McLeod. I guess you thought you'd seen the last of me. Me and the rest of Lilith's family."

Lacy heard the undercurrent of ugliness in the man's voice and remembered that Turner had said Anthony hated him. He had come a long way, and Lacy knew now it was not totally about trapping a white panther. Her pulse drummed and she felt as if she couldn't get a deep breath.

"What are you doing up here, Anthony?" Turner's voice was level. Not friendly, but not antagonistic.

"Looking for a white panther. There's a lot of money to be made from such a cat." He laughed. "Imagine, no one would know such a creature was here except for you."

The words were designed to make Turner angry, and Lacy reached over to softly touch his hand. It was exactly the wrong thing to do. The man stepped into the sunlight, his face bitter and furious.

"It didn't take you long to replace my sister after you killed her," he said, glaring at Lacy.

"This is a reporter, Lacy Wade," Turner said.

"I'm not stupid," Anthony replied with heat. "She's been staying at your cabin. I watch you, McLeod. I wait for you to make a big mistake, so I can be the one who gets the credit for bringing you down."

"Lacy is a friend," Turner said calmly. "She's working on a magazine piece. I'm sure she'd like to talk to you. She was headed for St. Martinsville to talk with your family."

"Right, and it's going to snow green tonight." Anthony's laugh was bitter. "You charmed an entire town, but you don't fool me. You killed my sister."

"I did not," Turner said sternly.

"She rejected you and you killed her!" Anthony was getting more and more worked up. "You couldn't stand it that she didn't want you."

"In your heart, Anthony, you know that isn't true. Lilith broke the engagement and asked me not to see her again. She asked me to leave town and I did. I was in LaFayette when the fire started."

"Turning tail and running is what you were doing. You were about to be arrested, and if some of your high-powered friends hadn't stepped in, you'd be rotting in jail right this minute."

"I'm innocent," Turner insisted, easing himself onto a large rock. "I should have stayed in town and proved it, but failure to do that is the only thing I've done wrong."

"How did you manage to get away without even being charged?" Anthony pressed. "Who did you pay? Who did you bribe with all your money?" His face was twisted with anger. "People like you think money cures everything. Well, it can't buy me off. I want justice."

Lacy thought about not saying anything at all. In Anthony's eyes, she was Lilith's competitor. To call attention to herself would only make worse trouble for Turner. But there was a chance she might be able to sway the enraged man. It was a risk, but she decided to take it.

"I want the same thing," she said, stepping well away from Turner just in case Anthony decided to shoot at her. "I'm writing an article about Turner, and I was sent here to find the truth."

"That's why you paid his bond?" Anthony scoffed. "Right, you're just an unbiased reporter."

"I paid his bond to keep him out of jail so he could prove his innocence," Lacy continued, forcing her voice to remain calm, reasonable, even though she was frightened half to death.

"He isn't innocent. He's guilty. He's a murderer and a fire starter, and he deserves to die." Anthony looked at Turner, and the barrel of his rifle swung from Lacy to him.

She held her breath, afraid to say more, afraid not to. Anthony was a man on the edge.

"I loved Lilith," Turner said in that calm voice that defied fear or panic. "I would never have hurt her. When she asked me to leave her alone, I did. I wanted to talk to her, to find out why she'd broken the engagement. But she asked me not to contact her, so I packed my things and left town. That's the truth, Anthony, whether you want to believe it or not. I was in LaFayette, drunk, when she died."

"You didn't have an alibi. The cops just believed you because you paid them."

Turner shook his head. "You're wrong on two counts. I don't have that kind of money, and not every cop can be bought off. It's probably a lot harder than you imagine."

"You're good at lying, aren't you?" Anthony countered.

"I'm telling the truth. Think about this. Would Lilith have wanted to marry me if I was a liar? Your sister wouldn't have tolerated lying. You know that as well as I do."

Anthony's mouth was hard. "And she changed her mind, didn't she. What did she learn about you that made you have to kill her?"

Lacy was appalled at the sudden turn in the conversation. Instead of helping himself, Turner was only digging himself in deeper. If this kept on much longer, the agitated man was going to kill them both.

"There are laws against stalking people," she said, forcing a change in topic.

"I'm not stalking anyone. I'm hunting a wild animal. One that's been spotted around here and may be a danger to the community. I'm doing a public service." Anthony seemed proud of his cover.

"You're holding a gun on two people who have done you no harm," Lacy said. "That's a crime."

"You were stealing my traps. I merely stopped two thieves in the middle of a theft."

Lacy felt her own temper rise. She started toward Anthony, and he swung the gun in her direction. The action stopped her in her tracks.

Another man stepped out of the woods behind Anthony. He, too, carried a high-powered rifle with a big scope. He walked up beside Anthony and put a hand on the younger man's shoulder. "So, they were stealing our traps," he said, his gaze roving over Lacy. "We got ourselves a couple of thieves. Now I'm wondering what we should do with them."

Lacy didn't recognize him. He bore a resemblance to the man who'd knocked her off M&M on the trail, and the way he was looking at her made her want to step close to Turner. She held her ground, unwilling to allow him to bully or intimidate her.

Instead, she studied him. Like Anthony he had dark hair and eyes and an olive complexion. Though the two men didn't appear related, they shared the same olive complexion.

"Who are you?" Turner asked, addressing the newcomer.

"An old family friend of Lilith and Anthony's." He grinned, and to Lacy his grin was more savage than Anthony's anger. "We heard about this white panther. Figured the hide and head would bring a lot, and times haven't been all that good down in St. Martinsville." His rifle barrel dropped to the ground. "Seen any signs of the big cat?"

Lacy wanted to put a hand on Turner, but she dared not. They were baiting Turner, going for him in a place where he had no defenses.

"I've seen no signs of anything around here except irresponsible trappers."

She gritted her teeth. Turner seemed determined to provoke the two men, and they had rifles.

Anthony's friend laughed. "Well, I don't think you'll be calling the game warden on us. I hear you've got your own troubles with the law. Arson charge, isn't it? Almost killed that young woman standing beside you." He stared at Lacy. "She's easy to look at, but not all that bright, eh?"

Turner did start forward, and Lacy grabbed the sleeve of his jacket. "Don't let him do that," she said. "He'll shoot you and claim self-defense." She wanted to remind Turner that he already had an arson charge against him. Some people might view his death as justice that didn't cost the taxpayer a dime.

Beneath her hand, she felt Turner's muscles, rigid with his desire to fight. He was a man with a slow fuse, but it was surely lit now. She had to do something to prevent the impending tragedy.

A noise in the distance caught her attention. Anthony and his friend heard it, too. They looked up, heads cocked. Lacy recognized the sound—chopper. Someone was flying over in a helicopter, and flying low.

"We're watching you, McLeod," Anthony said. Without preamble, he and his friend disappeared back into the woods as silently as they had arrived.

Turner put his arm around Lacy and pulled her to him. "The only thing that kept me from trying to kill them was the thought of what they might do to you," he said.

"Good thinking," she answered, finding the shelter of his arms the sweetest comfort she'd ever known. "I had a few concerns there myself."

She stepped back and looked up into the sky. The chopper was visible through the trees.

"Law enforcement," she said. "I think someone found an easier way to deliver your court date."

"I think we'll catch a ride down with them," he said. "I have enough hay stored under a tarp for three days for the horses. They have fresh water, and we can take Rex with us. Do you think we can find the answers to all of this in three days?''

''I don't know, but it's worth a try.''

''Running into Anthony here—I'm positive you're right, Lacy. The truth lies somewhere in Lilith's death. The things that have been happening are no coincidence, and if we don't learn the truth, eventually someone else is going to die.''

She started to tell him that the second man was the one who attacked her, but she was afraid it would send Turner after the two armed men. She decided the best thing to do was retain that bit of information, at least for the time being.

THE DEPUTY WAS CURIOUS and courteous as he explained that Turner needed to be in court at nine the next morning. It was an arraignment, something of a formality, but Turner had to be there. At the clearing where the chopper landed Turner broached the subject of a ride down the mountain for Lacy, the dog and him, the deputy never hesitated.

''I'd hate to have to walk back up here to get you,'' Brad Welford said. ''You're welcome to a ride down.''

Turner hurriedly put together his things for the trip as Lacy put the three remaining bales of hay in the corral for the horses and made sure the watering trough was filled. She hated the idea of leaving them alone, especially knowing that Anthony and his friend were in the area. But there seemed no alternative.

The deputy had landed the helicopter in a nearby clearing, exactly the one that Lacy had determined would be a good drop site for supplies. When she mentioned the idea to the deputy, he quickly gave her the name of a private service that made airdrops. Lacy wrote it down, along with the deputy's name. She was determined to have a list of things ready for delivery when they headed back to the cabin—after they'd proved Turner innocent of his charges.

Deputy Welford set them down as close to the roadside park where they'd left the Suburban as he could. Then he was gone, with a reminder that court was at nine in the morning.

Lacy and Turner, with Rex in the back seat, drove into Claytonville and checked into a motel where no one would notice Rex.

"What now?" Lacy said as she sat on the king-size bed.

Turner looked at her and had definite ideas about what they could do. But he wanted a future with Lacy, not a few stolen hours in a motel. To get what he wanted, he had to prove himself innocent. For the first time in years, he actually cared what people thought of him. He had to care—or else Lacy would be lost to him.

"I need to buy a suit," he said. It had been years since he'd worn anything other than jeans and flannel shirts. "I want to make a good impression in court tomorrow. And I guess I'd better start checking into hiring a lawyer."

He saw the happiness on her face. He was beginning to fight, and she was proud of him.

"I want to go to the library and see if I can find anything on the Internet about Lilith's death." She'd learned a few research tools in college. Anything they learned before they got to St. Martinsville would cut the time they had to spend there—and they didn't have time to waste.

"We'll meet back here for dinner," he said, his gaze straying over the bed.

It was almost as if Lacy read his mind. She stood up and came to him, her arms circling his neck as she pressed herself against him.

"You have to have witnesses to everywhere you go," she reminded him. "Get the name of the sales-clerks. Get them to write down the time you were in the store."

He could tell she was dead serious, and she was also right. She was his alibi, and he had a feeling he was going to need one.

"Documented to the last second," he assured her.

"We'll get everything done that we can, and then we'll come back here tonight and make the most of what time we have," she whispered in his ear.

Turner enfolded her in his arms. He meant his kiss to be restrained, more of a thank-you than an invitation. But kissing Lacy simply wasn't something he could do with a lot of restraint. No matter how noble his intentions, once he had her in his arms, his desire for her became all-consuming.

He forced himself to draw away from her responsive kisses. "Lacy," he said softly against her hair.

"I know," she answered, sighing as she pressed her face against his chest. "I had no idea," she said, "what it could feel like to want someone so. Turner, what am I going to do if you can't prove you're innocent?"

It was the question he needed to push him into action. "We can't let that happen. I never worried that prison would be too much for me. I guess that was because I was already in prison—emotional prison. But now that I've tasted what freedom is with you, I can't go back to being so alone.''

''I know,'' she said, looking up into his eyes. ''I feel exactly the same way.''

Chapter Thirteen

It took help from a friendly librarian, but Lacy was able to access the local newspaper files from St. Martinsville. The coverage of Lilith's murder was extensive and sad. Lacy had mixed feelings, reading about Lilith's kind nature and beloved status.

The details of the fire were what she sought, and the small weekly newspaper had given them lots of space. As Turner said, the fire had started in the attic of the house. The assumption by the fire chief was that it was old wiring in an old house. The attic had been filled with trunks of clothes and memorabilia, the perfect place for a stray spark to ignite.

The unsolved element of the fire was why Lilith had not escaped. Fire detectors should have awakened her. The owner of the local hardware store was quoted as saying that Lilith had talked to him about the installation of the detectors within the past ten months.

Lacy made notes as she read the newspaper account. When she was finished, she knew little more than she had before. Turner's name was mentioned by the local sheriff, and there was another story that said he had been questioned and released.

Ultimately the fire was ruled accidental.

She scrolled through several more months of the newspaper, but found no other mention of the fire. What she did have was a list of people to talk with once she got to St. Martinsville. And she was leaving none of it to chance. Using the cell phone that was useless in the wilderness, she called the sheriff, the fire chief and several of the neighbors who were quoted in the article and made appointments to talk with all of them when she got to town. She also called Erin Brown at *Texas Legends*. The editor was eager for her story, but Lacy managed to hold her off.

That done, she walked back to the motel to wait for Turner.

There was a message for her. Turner had called from a lawyer's office, saying he would be detained.

"I've hired Ray Mennon. He's familiar with the fire in Crossroads. He has a cousin who lives there. We're going over to the courthouse to talk with the deputies now."

Lacy sat down in the middle of the bed with her notepad and began to rank the people she wanted to interview in order of importance. When the door to the room opened, at first she didn't recognize the man who walked into the room.

She let out a long low whistle of appreciation. "Call Oprah. I think you're a perfect candidate for a make-over show," she said, standing and walking around him. The suit was perfectly cut, as was his hair. It was Turner, but Turner looking a way she'd never seen. "Wow. Very handsome. Very Wall Street."

Even Rex walked around him, sniffing as if to be sure this man was indeed his master.

"I got something for you, too," he said, stepping

back outside the door and bringing in a black clothes bag with gold lettering on it. "I wasn't sure you'd have a chance to shop before tomorrow, so I took the liberty of picking out a dress."

Lacy took the bag with a trembling hand. It had been many many years since someone had picked out something for her. "I don't know what to say, Turner."

"'Thank you' will do perfectly." He held the hanger while she opened the bag, revealing a dark-green dress. It was beautifully made, a dress that was all about class.

"It's lovely." She unzipped it and put it on the bed. "I should try it on."

"Yes, I'd like that."

His smile made her blush. "I've been out tracking down your past, and all you've been doing is thinking about—"

"—making love to you. Is that what you were going to accuse me of? Then I plead guilty to that charge. We can skip the whole court matter and I'll just tell them I'm as guilty as I can be."

Lacy knew flattery when she heard it, and she loved every second of it. She stepped out of her jeans, slowly unbuttoned her shirt and tossed it on the bed. Turner watched her and she could almost feel his touch on her body, moving over her. She stepped into the dress. It was a perfect fit, as if someone had designed it especially for her.

Turner fastened the zipper and then turned her so he could see. "I never realized before what excellent taste I have in women's clothes. And in women." He turned her around so she could see herself in the mirror.

The dress was wonderful, but Lacy was caught by
the reflection of the two of them together. They both
looked as if they belonged in the clothes they wore—
and as if they belonged together. They could wear
potato sacks and it wouldn't make any difference.
What Lacy saw in the man standing beside her was
the man she had somehow, against all logic, fallen in
love with.

"You've obviously bought suits before today," she
said, searching for something to say.

"I've worked wearing a suit every day—I just prefer to wear something else," he said, hugging her
against him. "Or maybe nothing at all."

Lacy wanted only his embrace. She leaned into
him. "I bought a suit for my job interview at the
magazine. I've worn it once," she said.

"I hope we can hang our suits side by side and
never have to worry about putting them on again for
the rest of our lives."

It was a sweet throwaway comment, but one that
Lacy took straight to her heart. Turner wasn't offering
her a future, but he also wasn't running from the idea
of her still with him down the road. It was no dec-
laration of love, but it was something pretty special.

She slipped her arms around his neck, lifting her
lips for his kiss. Even if tonight was her last night
with Turner, she would take it with a glad heart.

His kiss was dizzying. More than anything, Lacy
wanted to be able to make love to Turner knowing
that tomorrow they would have another day together,
another week, another month. None of that was true.

She had to snatch what happiness she could. And
she didn't hesitate. She felt Turner's fingers at her
back, slowly unzipping the dress. She let it fall down

her body, catching it with one finger so that it wouldn't wrinkle.

Easing back from him, she gave him an inviting look. "Take off your suit," she said. "I think we should take advantage of this very large bed."

"I like the way you think," Turner replied, undressing as he spoke.

She knew he was worried about the future, but the one gift she could give him was a night of forgetfulness. That was exactly what she intended to do.

THE ARRAIGNMENT WENT just as Turner's lawyer predicted. Turner pleaded not guilty and was bound over to the grand jury. As Turner had feared, it was a heyday for the media. Camera crews were set up everywhere, and the story of a "fire starter" was gossiped about in shouts and whispers up and down the courthouse square.

Lacy was his only consolation. She stuck by his side like glue, whispering at him to ignore the questions hurled at him from reporters who were only doing their jobs.

"Is it true, Mr. McLeod, that as a young child you could make your teacher's desk burst into flame?" one young man asked, shoving a microphone into Turner's face.

Lacy grabbed the microphone. "That's the most ridiculous question I've ever heard. Don't you think if that was true, Turner would be some kind of secret government weapon by now?"

Turner hid his smile. The situation wasn't funny, but Lacy's indignation was amusing. The shoe was now on the other foot. She was experiencing firsthand the reason he'd been reluctant to be interviewed.

They escaped the courthouse and Turner was about to give a sigh of relief when he saw Sheriff Taylor waiting for him on the lawn. There were four television cameras, reporters and several still photographers behind him.

Turner recognized an ambush when he saw one, as did Lacy. She instinctively began to cut back. Behind them was another pack of media.

"Come on," he said, taking her elbow. "You're about to blow your credibility as an unbiased reporter."

"At this point I'm not really worried about that," she said.

The sheriff stepped toward Turner. "I've been looking into your past, Mr. McLeod. You might have gotten away with arson and murder in Louisiana, but you won't do it here in Brisco County, Texas."

"Instead of manipulating the media, Sheriff, I'd be more concerned about proving your case. There is no evidence to connect me to that fire. I'm innocent."

"I just wanted to make sure you understood that we serve up justice in Brisco County, and the good people here can't be bought." Sheriff Taylor looked into the television cameras as he spoke.

"Sheriff, I think you should consider the consequences of accusing a man in public." He felt Lacy's fingers dig into his arm. Looking quickly at her, he saw concern in her eyes.

"Is that a threat, Mr. McLeod?" the sheriff asked.

Turner was about to answer when he saw someone at the back of the crowd. Anthony was smiling at him, a look of satisfaction on his face. Now Turner knew what had gotten the sheriff so fired up.

"I don't make threats," Turner said. "I only meant

that slander can sometimes carry a hefty price tag.''
Again he felt Lacy's fingers, warning him to be careful of what he said.

He was all too aware that the television cameras were rolling, taking in every word he uttered. And he had made a mistake, one he couldn't talk his way out of. To try to explain that he was referring to civil consequences would only make it worse.

As Lacy discreetly tugged on his arm, he followed her away from the cameras. When he looked back over his shoulder, Anthony had stepped up to the sheriff and they were talking.

"Did you see Anthony there?" he asked Lacy as they climbed into the Suburban.

"I did. He's determined to make trouble for you, Turner. As much trouble as he can."

He could see she was very worried. "I wasn't threatening the sheriff."

"I know that and you know that, but I can only imagine how it's going to sound on the news tonight. You have to be more careful."

"Maybe I need some coaching," he said, only half joking.

"Now that's something I can help you with," Lacy said, nodding her head. "We'll work on this while we're driving to Louisiana."

"The good thing about Anthony being in town is that he isn't up around the cabin and the horses," Turner said.

"Yes, every cloud has a silver lining, as my grandmother would say."

LACY WAS UNPREPARED for the charm of the small Louisiana town. Even though Turner was supposed to

remain in Brisco County, they had decided to risk the
long drive. Lacy was certain the answers lay in
Turner's past, and she intended to unearth them.

For all of the town's charm, Lacy knew that Turner
was not welcome there. Two women passed by them,
casting hostile looks at Turner. It had been three years
since Lilith's death, but no one seemed to have forgotten—or forgiven—Turner. It didn't matter that
he'd never been charged; the fact that he'd been questioned was enough. The town needed someone to
blame, and he had been the unusual outsider, the man
who'd come into town and swept the local princess
off her feet.

The dynamics of the story would make one helluva
book, Lacy thought with a strange tingle of emotion.
She gave Turner a wry smile as they walked side by
side to the newspaper office.

"What's so amusing?" he asked, nodding to a man
they passed. The man gave him a look of dislike and
crossed the street.

"I was just thinking this would make a terrific
book. Pretty ambitious for a writer who hasn't even
written her first magazine article."

"I hope you aren't just using me," Turner said.

Lacy stopped him and searched his face. "I hope
that was a joke."

He nodded. "It was. But you should know, this is
very difficult. To come back here, to remember it all
again. I'd hoped to put all of this behind me."

There was such pain in Turner's voice that Lacy
considered getting back into the Suburban and leaving. What if they accomplished nothing here? All of
this pain would be to no good end.

Turner took her hand. "There's the newspaper. Earl Spriggs is the editor."

"I spoke with him last night," Lacy reminded Turner. "He's expecting us."

"He'll want to do an interview."

"No doubt," she agreed. "I certainly would. We just have to be very careful of what we say and hope he isn't so careful."

Lacy wasn't surprised that Earl Spriggs was cool toward them. Like everyone else in town, he assumed Turner was somehow to blame for a death and had escaped punishment.

"Is there anything else you can tell us that wasn't in the newspaper?" Lacy asked, notebook in hand.

"Mr. McLeod would seem to be the man with the answers," Earl said meaningfully.

"I told Sheriff Dodds everything," Turner said. "I told the truth."

The editor gave him a long look. "Why are you here? You weren't interested in talking to me three years ago."

"I'm accused of being a fire starter. I'm innocent. I want to prove that I wasn't responsible for Lilith's death or for any other fire," Turner said.

Lacy could have kissed him. He was so honest, trying so hard to tell the truth.

"Lilith's family still believes you had something to do with her death. It's torn that family apart. Her brother, Anthony, quit his job. He's become something of a recluse."

Turner thought for a moment. "Anthony has been following me. I know he feels he has a right to do whatever he can to hurt me because he believes I hurt someone he loves. I hope Lacy and I can figure out what really happened and bring some peace to Anthony and the rest of that family."

Earl nodded. "I wish you'd talked to me when this happened."

Turner stood up. "I do, too. Hindsight is always twenty-twenty, Mr. Spriggs. If you think of something that may help us discover what really happened, please call."

Lacy pulled a business card with her cell-phone number from her purse. "If you think of any little thing," she said as they left.

The interview with Toby Dodds, the parish sheriff, was much the same. At first he was cool, but as Turner and Lacy explained themselves, he warmed to them.

"Lilith's death has troubled me," he confessed. "Why didn't she wake up and save herself? That's the question that has always haunted me."

"Was there anyone else who might have wanted her hurt?" Lacy asked, drawing looks from both men. "Since Turner didn't have anything to do with it, if there was foul play, someone had to be responsible."

Toby shook his head. "Hard to believe anyone would hurt Lilith. There were always men who pursued her, but she was never unkind. That was the thing about her. She treated everyone with respect, even those she disliked."

"And were there people she disliked?" Lacy pressed.

"A beautiful woman always has unwanted suitors. Back before she started seeing Mr. McLeod, there were a couple of men who couldn't seem to take no for an answer. Once Mr. McLeod was on the scene, though, they gave it up. Or at least, she never mentioned them to me again.''

"Do you know the names of those men?" Lacy asked.

The sheriff looked uncomfortable. "I don't want to see people made to look bad in a magazine piece. *Texas Legends* doesn't have the best reputation as far as truth and honesty go, Ms. Wade. I won't tell you the names, but I promise I'll do some checking into it."

"And if you find anything, you'll let me know, right?" Lacy handed him one of her cards.

"You have my word."

Turner stood up. "Sheriff Dodds, I loved Lilith. I would never have hurt her. I loved her enough to leave when she asked me. I'm innocent of the accusations that have been made, and I'm going to prove it. I believe you'll help me find the truth."

"That's my job, McLeod."

"Then we're on the same team." Turner took Lacy's arm as they left the office.

Dusk was falling by the time they got outside. Rex was waiting in the truck, and they got in and drove to the small bed-and-breakfast where they'd reserved a room.

"We have to go back tomorrow," Turner said. "The horses will need attention."

"I know," Lacy said. She was discouraged and doing her best not to show it. "Lilith must have been a saint. She didn't have enemies. She was kind." Lacy got out of the truck and went into the cottage. It was only twenty yards from Bayou Teche.

Turner came up behind her and touched her shoulders, massaging lightly. "She was a good person."

"Why didn't she wake up?" Lacy said, despair in her voice. "Would someone have hurt her to get at you?"

Turner's hands stopped on her shoulders. When she turned around to look at him, he was pale.

"Someone would have to hate me a lot to kill an innocent woman."

Lacy knew she had to tread carefully here. "Turner, when we first met, you were pretty hard-nosed. I know you haven't hurt anyone, but..." She let the sentence hang.

"But you think because I wouldn't defend myself, someone might have thought I did something."

"And built up a good case, at least in his or her mind, that you deserved punishing."

"But to set fire to a woman's house?"

"Maybe they didn't mean to actually hurt her." She took a breath. "This wasn't the first time you were framed."

Turner came and sat beside her. "You're right. But who could hate me enough to spend their life following me around, trying to set me up for a prison sentence?"

"That's a question I can't answer."

"Nor can I at the moment. But I'll think about it."

That was the most that Lacy could hope. Turner would think about it. He had to. Their time was running out.

There was a tap at the door, and she went to answer it. The attractive woman who ran the bed-and-breakfast was standing there, shifting her weight from foot to foot. Her mouth was a thin line.

"Sheriff Dodds is up at the house looking for you."

Lacy's face lit up. "Maybe he has some news."

"I knew I shouldn't have rented this to you," the woman said, wringing her hands. "I thought I remembered your name. You're the man who was involved with that fire. And now they're hunting for you in Texas for trying to burn down the sheriff of Brisco County's home."

Lacy felt as if she'd been punched in the stomach. "What?"

The woman looked scared, but she was also angry. "You can't go all over the country burning people out. Sheriff Dodds is here to take you in. He said to tell you to come along peacefully."

Turner put a hand on Lacy's shoulder to keep her quiet. "The sheriff sent you here to tell us?"

Lacy realized how strange an action that truly was. The sheriff had sent someone to... warn them?

"Sheriff Dodds said for you to get your things together and come in peacefully. He's not in the mood for any shenanigans."

"Tell him I'm on the way," Turner said. "I need to gather our things."

The woman nodded. "He said you'd be cooperative." She turned and left without a backward glance.

"What's going on?" Lacy asked as soon as she was sure the woman was out of earshot.

"For some strange reason, Sheriff Dodds is giving us a chance to make a getaway. I don't know how or why, but I think we should take it."

"What could have happened in Claytonville?" Lacy asked. "It sounded like the Sheriff Taylor's house burned."

"We need to find that out as soon as we can. But

this time, Lacy, I have something I've never had before."

"What?" she asked.

"You. I couldn't have started this fire. Except for the time I spent yesterday, which is documented, you've been with me every moment since we came down from the cabin."

Chapter Fourteen

They were exhausted when they finally stopped at a convenience store for something to eat. Lacy went in, loading up with bottled water, sandwiches and all the newspapers she could find. The fire in Brisco County was big news in all of them.

Turner's picture was on the front page of two papers, and hers was prominently featured on the inside. It was just a lucky break that the young salesclerk didn't recognize her.

Turner was driving, and when he turned off the main road to Claytonville, Lacy sat up straight. "Where are you going?" she asked. She handed the last of a sandwich to Rex, who seemed to enjoy chicken salad and rides in a vehicle.

"I'm not sure."

"You should go straight to the courthouse and turn yourself in. We can prove you're innocent this time," she argued. "That's why Sheriff Dodds didn't arrest you, Turner. He was giving you a chance to prove you were innocent."

"I'm not so certain your word is going to be enough to save me," he said slowly.

"It's enough. You have to do this."

He shook his head. "I don't think it's the right move."

Lacy did her best to fight back the sense of panic. "Turner, you're a fugitive. The newspaper accounts implied that I might be with you against my will. If the wrong person sees you, he might decide that he's doing a public service if he 'brings you to justice.'"

She didn't have to point out that Anthony would be more than glad to ruin Turner.

"Call the sheriff and tell him you were with me. See what happens."

It was a very good idea, and Lacy made the call on her cell phone. Although it was early in the morning, Sheriff Taylor quickly got on the line.

"Sheriff, this is Lacy Wade."

"Where are you?" The sheriff was instantly alert.

"I'm fine. Turner didn't have a thing to do with your house burning. He was with me the entire time. We weren't even close to Claytonville."

"I don't know why you'd want to lie for that man, Ms. Wade, but if you have any influence on him, convince him to turn himself in. If he doesn't, I can't say what will happen to him. Folks around here are pretty stirred up."

"Sheriff, Turner has been framed. I'm telling you he was with me and had nothing to do with a fire."

"If he's innocent, he can prove it," the sheriff said.

"He shouldn't have to prove his innocence," Lacy said, feeling her own temper start a slow burn. "We want to cooperate, but it sounds as if he's already been convicted."

"That man all but threatened to burn me out. And now my home is destroyed. This has nearly killed my wife. She's heartbroken."

Lacy knew he was angry and upset, but blaming Turner wasn't the answer.

"Turner is innocent."

"I can't take your word for that, Ms. Wade. I have to tell you, you're aiding and abetting a wanted man. You're putting yourself in a serious position."

"I'm defending an innocent man," Lacy said. "I'm telling you the truth. Turner was with me. He wasn't involved in the fire. Somehow we'll prove it." She disconnected.

There was silence for a few moments before Turner spoke. "I gather from what I heard he wasn't interested in hearing that I had an alibi."

"He wasn't." Lacy didn't know what to do. If Turner turned himself in, there seemed a good chance he would be railroaded. His words to the sheriff had been broadcast on a lot of television stations, and someone who didn't know Turner could easily have construed what he said as a threat. There was an explanation, but would anyone listen?

"What are we going to do?" Lacy asked.

"We?"

She nodded. "I'm not about to drop out now."

He reached across the seat and picked up her hand. "I don't know what I did to deserve you, but I can only say thank-you. Are you sure, though, Lacy? After that conversation with the sheriff, he knows you're with me by choice. Your future is as much on the line as mine is."

Lacy knew all that Turner said was true. This was a moment from which there was no turning back. She was binding her future to a man she'd known for a short time, but in that time, she'd grown to love him. She'd learned to believe in him and to trust him.

"I don't know about the future," she finally said. "I only know about right now. I believe you're innocent. That's something worth fighting for."

"Okay," he said, squeezing her hand. "Thank you, Lacy. If you believe I'm worth fighting for, then I'm going to fight. This time I won't walk away."

"This time you can't, Turner," Lacy said softly.

"Even if I could, I'd stay and fight because I know if I didn't, I'd lose you."

He took a right turn down a narrow county road.

"Where are we going?" she asked.

"My guess is that Anthony is behind the fire at the sheriff's. I think he may have been behind all the fires since Lilith's death. I'm going to find him."

"Where? How?" she asked.

"He's out to set me up as an arsonist. I may be wrong, but I think he's gone back to the cabin. He's got everyone hunting me, believing I'm some kind of fiend. Now he's probably planting the evidence that will prove my guilt."

The words chilled Lacy to the bone. "He may be responsible for the fires since Lilith's death, but what about the others?" she asked. "There was that fire in Pablo. What happened?"

Turner concentrated on the road for several miles. "It was the local high-school principal's home. I was teaching there and I had a disagreement with the man. He thought that by teaching the old legends and folklore that I was somehow influencing the students to believe in magic."

"Ridiculous," Lacy said.

"Yes, ridiculous, but a very serious issue to him."

"So what happened?"

"I agreed to finish out the year and leave. It was a decision that was mutually satisfying."

"And the fire?"

"I don't know. There were only five weeks left in school at the time we had our discussion. A week later his home burned."

"And again there was no evidence to connect you to the fire?"

"None. But the rumors started all over again. I was a fire starter. I was a man who settled an argument with flames."

"And you left."

Again it was several moments before Turner spoke. "Yes, I left. It seemed easier to leave than to stay and try to prove I was innocent. There was no legal charge, so I left."

"What about the other fires?" Lacy said. She didn't want to force Turner to talk, but she knew she had to. The answer to who was starting the fires was somewhere. They hadn't found it in St. Martinsville, but it had to be somewhere in the past.

"There were two others. One when I just got out of college, another when I was doing some research in a small town called Jackson Creek."

"Same story?"

"Pretty much. In college I had a disagreement with a teacher. His garage burned. Gas leak in the car, no proof that it was set. But my guess was that someone cut the fuel line, waited for enough fuel to spill beneath the car, and then set it. No charges, but I had been at his home that night. Our discussion had gotten loud. In Jackson Creek, a co-worker's office burned. No one was ever injured. Except Lilith."

"But how did the fire-starter rumor begin?"

"I don't know. I never told anyone about my family's tragedy. It was something I hated to talk about. I really only wanted to forget it, to develop my life and keep moving forward. But after Professor Brent's garage burned, the rumor started."

There was so much pain in Turner's voice that Lacy slid across the seat and leaned her head on his shoulder. "I'm so sorry."

"Me, too. But the rumor got all over campus that I had burned Dr. Brent's garage and that I had actually set the fire that ended up killing my brother. It was so awful I dropped out of that school and took off a year. That's when I became interested in myths and legends. It was a good excuse to spend a lot of time alone, uninvolved with people who might get hurt by contact with me."

Lacy leaned up and kissed his cheek. He had finally opened up to her, told her about the past. It was a big step in building a future, for himself and for them together. "You don't hurt people, Turner. You can't believe that."

"People get hurt when they get too close to me. That's an indisputable fact."

"Another way of looking at it is that someone is hurting the people you care about. Someone is deliberately hurting them—to hurt you."

Turner slammed the steering wheel hard. "Who would do that? Why? Why would a person hate me that much?"

"You'd better think hard," Lacy said. "Someone hates you a lot. And that someone is pretty damn smart."

TURNER PULLED THE TRUCK off the road and down a narrow lane that was barely visible. Lacy thought of the long hike ahead of them and wanted to groan. One thing, when this was over, she'd be in the best physical shape she'd ever been.

"How are we going up?" she asked.

"The sheriff's deputy gave you the number for an independent helicopter service, didn't he?"

Lacy felt a surge of hope. "We're flying up?"

Turner nodded. "Keep your fingers crossed that he isn't booked. We're out of time. Call the place. Tell him to pick us up at Leopold's Cave. He'll know where it is, and there's a perfect spot for him to land."

"What about Rex?" Lacy said.

"We'll deal with it at the time if there's a problem."

"When do you want him to meet us?" Lacy asked.

"The sooner the better. Tell him it's a cash deal, whatever he asks."

Lacy wasted no time digging the number out of her wallet and calling the service. She had the pilot booked and ready to go in the next hour. Even though Turner didn't tell her, she decided to use her grandmother's name to book the flight.

"Let's just hope he isn't a man who pays a lot of attention to the news," Turner said.

"Are you feeling lucky?" Lacy quipped halfheartedly.

"A lot luckier since I met you." He motioned her out of the truck. "It's about a thirty-minute walk. They'll eventually find the Suburban, but by then we'll be at the cabin."

"And then what?" Lacy asked.

"We find Anthony."

"Even if Anthony is responsible for the latest fires, it still doesn't explain the ones before you knew Lilith," Lacy pointed out for the second time.

"I know, but it's a beginning," Turner said. "And it's the only idea I have right now." He put his arm around Lacy and hugged her. "I'm open to any suggestions at any time."

They made the hike in just thirty minutes, and it wasn't long before they heard the helicopter headed their way. The pilot set the bird down and they ran toward it, ducking the blades as they climbed aboard.

To Turner's relief, the pilot paid more attention to the money he handed him than he did to his passengers—especially Rex, who boarded as if flying in a helicopter was an everyday part of his life.

In only minutes they were up and soaring over the wilderness, headed toward the isolated area where the cabin was located. Turner directed him to the same clearing the sheriff's deputy had used for a landing zone. They got out of the helicopter and watched the pilot take off again.

"Now we have to find Anthony," Turner said, striking off for the cabin.

"How?" Lacy asked.

"With any luck, he'll come to us."

LACY WAS RELIEVED to see both horses in the corral as they finally entered the small clearing around the cabin. Turner checked the horses' water as Lacy went inside. She stopped in the doorway. Someone had been in the cabin and trashed it. All of Turner's possessions where thrown around the small enclosure. His research papers were scattered and half destroyed. The sight made her heartsick.

She stepped outside. "I'm afraid we're too late. Someone's already been here."

Turner walked to the door and looked in. He seemed to have no reaction, not even anger.

He walked in and picked up a sheaf of papers. "My search for the white panther seems to have gotten lost in all my personal problems," he said.

"When this is over, you can still search for him," Lacy said, wanting to offer what little comfort she could.

"Sometimes it seems my whole life has been a search for the impossible. Maybe clearing my name is just another impossible dream."

Lacy understood what Turner had to be feeling, but she couldn't let him give up hope. "We'll prove your innocence, Turner. We don't have time for you to doubt yourself now. How long do you think we have before they come looking for you here?"

"Not long," he said.

"So what's the plan?"

He began gathering the papers and stacking them, along with his books and the pieces of equipment. "I think we have to set a trap."

Lacy didn't like the sound of that, but she didn't have a better idea. "How?"

"If I'm correct, Anthony is probably still watching the cabin. I think we should stage a fight. You saddle M&M and pretend to leave."

"What will that do?" She didn't like the idea of leaving Turner. "I'm your alibi, remember? What if another fire starts and I'm an hour down the trail?"

Turner put a hand on her shoulder. "Lacy, if Anthony sees you leave, he may come after me. This is between us. I'm going to saddle Buster and pretend that I'm leaving—that I'm running away. Anthony won't be able to resist trying to stop me." He tightened his grip on her shoulder, using his strong fingers to gently massage. "As long as you're right here, he'll hold back. We don't have a lot of time."

"Why did you bring me back up here if you're only going to send me away?" she asked.

"You'll only be down the trail. I can send Rex to get you once I capture Anthony."

"What about his friend?" Lacy asked.

"This is between Anthony and me. I can manage both of them, if I have to. But it won't come to that."

Lacy felt a knot of dread in her stomach. "I don't think this is a good plan."

"It's not the best idea I've ever had, but it's the best I can come up with right now." He pinned her with his gaze. "Do you have a better suggestion?"

Lacy shook her head. She didn't. The difference between her and Turner was that she wanted to keep him safe. Drawing Anthony out was not a safe occupation. But it was essential. If they could only convince Anthony to tell the truth about the fire in Claytonville, then Turner could pursue the truth of the other fires in a more reasonable, safer way.

"Okay," she said. "But I don't think this is good."

"It probably isn't, but we're out of choices."

Lacy felt tears sting her eyes. The idea of riding off without Turner was awful. She grabbed for the jacket she'd just taken off. "It's freezing out there," she said.

He picked up his jacket, which he'd draped over a chair. "Take this. I have another one." He held it so that she could slip it on. "Ride for about half an hour.

You won't be that far away, and I'll send Rex for you. Before dark.'' He kissed her forehead. "I promise.''

Lacy raised her lips to his. "Be careful, Turner,'' she said. "Promise me?''

"I promise,'' he said, kissing her one last time. "Now, are you ready to be an actress?''

She nodded.

"Give it everything you've got,'' he said.

She picked up the small pack she'd prepared and walked to the door. Taking a deep breath, she turned back to him. "You're a stubborn arrogant fool!'' she yelled. "I'm going back to town and you can rot up here in your cabin!''

"All you ever wanted was a story!'' Turner countered loudly. "I'll saddle your horse. The quicker you're gone, the better for both of us. I should have known never to trust a reporter!''

"I'll leave, Turner, but this story isn't over. If I don't get it, someone else will. You should have told me about your past.''

"My past is nobody's business but my own!'' he snapped as he caught M&M and saddled him. In a moment he had the gelding bridled, and he led him over to Lacy. He grasped her waist and lifted her into the saddle, his hand lingering for just a moment.

"Be careful,'' he whispered, his lips brushing her thigh.

"You be careful,'' she returned, almost choking on her tears.

"Good riddance!'' he yelled as he lightly slapped M&M's rump and sent the horse down the trail.

Lacy didn't look back. She couldn't bear to. She looked at her watch and kicked the horse into a trot while the trail was still level. She had to make it look as if she was really leaving—and in a hurry.

Brushing the tears from her eyes, she sat erect in the saddle, just the way an angry woman would sit. There was nothing to do but play the role Turner had assigned her and trust him to do what he'd set out to do. By nightfall, she'd have her answer, and perhaps both she and Turner could come in from the cold.

Chapter Fifteen

Although the sun was still bright, Lacy was chilled to the bone after half an hour's ride. She halted M&M, dismounted and stamped her feet to bring the circulation back. Turning up the collar of Turner's jacket, she snuggled deeper into the fleece lining. She closed her eyes and remembered him, his touch and smell, the way he made her feel. It was almost enough to keep her going.

M&M shifted away from her, and Lacy reached down to pick up the reins. The last thing she needed was the horse taking off without her. Then she'd be stranded in the wilderness—again.

Knowing Anthony and his friend were somewhere about, Lacy couldn't help checking over her shoulder. She hadn't been able to positively identify Anthony's friend as the man who'd attacked her, but she would have bet a week's salary on it. If she had a salary. Once word got back to *Texas Legends* editor Erin Brown that Lacy had allied herself with Turner McLeod in the face of arson charges, Lacy knew her brief tenure at the magazine would be over. *Texas Legends* had never made a big point of being strict about facts, but to aid and abet a wanted man went over the line, even for that magazine. The truth was, she was getting a real story now. She would have to convince Erin when Turner had safely proved his innocence.

There had been no other choice but to help Turner. Once she'd given Turner her heart, the rest of her followed. What was it that made Turner not defend himself? she wondered. He'd never made an attempt to disavow the charges against him. He'd simply walked away. Why?

Although Turner figured the answer to the recent fires lay in Anthony, Lacy was more inclined to try to figure out why Turner had been so willing to let others believe him guilty. The problem was, she couldn't answer that question. Only Turner could, and even though he'd begun to open up a little about the facts of the past, he still wasn't forthcoming about his feelings.

She pulled the jacket he'd lent her closer around her neck and chest. Something rustled in the inside pocket. Reaching in, she pulled out a pale sheet of paper. Lacy knew without looking that it was a woman's note. It was a single sheet, folded once, and as she held it, the paper fluttered open. Lilith's signature was a bold scrawl at the bottom of the page.

The signature was like an alarm bell. Lacy's hand trembled as she began to read the words that Lilith had written to Turner.

The accusation was clear—as was the sadness that Lilith felt at what she obviously considered Turner's betrayal of her love. There was so much pain in the note that Lacy swallowed and closed her eyes. "Breathe," she said to herself. "Breathe slowly."

She took several deep breaths before she looked at the note again.

Nothing had changed. The second reading only made it worse. Knowing that the woman who'd written the note had burned to death was almost more than Lacy could bear. And knowing that Turner had kept the note from her made Lacy suddenly unsure of him.

She had risked everything. Her career, her future with the magazine and, most important of all, her heart. She had put all that on the line by believing in Turner. And he hadn't been truthful with her. How long had he had this note? She examined it. Not long. It was still neat and clean, the edges sharp. It would have been more frayed and battered if he'd been carrying it for long. But Lilith had been dead for three years. Turner hadn't carried the note in this jacket for that long.

So where had it come from?

She looked around, a chill touching her spine. Had Anthony delivered it to Turner? Was this the reason Anthony hated Turner so deeply? Whereas before she'd considered Anthony's anger at Turner to be misplaced grief, she now considered that he might have a reason. The note was one of the most damning things she'd ever seen.

And if Turner was truly innocent, why had he withheld the note from her?

Tears stung her eyes as she realized the extent of his betrayal. The future that she'd so happily envisioned crumbled around her. There could be no future with a man she didn't trust.

She gathered up M&M's reins. She had three choices. She could continue on down the trail, knowing that she'd spend at least one night camped on the ground. She could go back to Turner's cabin and confront him. Or she could simply wait until he sent Rex to retrieve her, as they'd planned.

Swinging up into the saddle, she still wasn't sure what to do. It was only when M&M turned and headed back toward the cabin that she decided. She would confront Turner. She would give him the chance to explain the note and his silence about it. Then she would decide what to do.

She felt a moment of bitter irony. Several times Turner had emphasized that Lilith had never told him why she'd changed her mind about loving him. Well, he wouldn't have the same complaint of her. She was going to tell him how his actions made her feel. How his betrayal tore at her heart.

TURNER TIED THE BEDROLL to the back of Buster's saddle. He had to make it look as if he was leaving for good. He'd had no indication that Anthony was actually watching him, but his instincts told him he'd calculated correctly. Anthony was somewhere nearby, waiting for his opportunity to strike. Turner had studied the trapper mentality for the past ten years, and he'd staked a lot on the belief that Anthony would act true to his hunter ways. Like so many of his friends, Anthony had grown up hunting and fishing. In Anthony's mind, the snare was neatly set around Turner, and Anthony wasn't about to let his prey escape.

Turner swung into the saddle and headed out. Now he had to remain alert. When Anthony came at him, it was going to be an ambush.

He took a trail that led back into the wilderness.

He'd scouted it earlier when he'd been hunting for the white panther. That seemed a lifetime ago. In a few short days, his world had been turned topsy-turvy.

Worry about Lacy ate at him. She was alone on the trail, and though he'd done everything he knew to keep her safe, she was as much a target as he was. He could only hope that the little scene they'd concocted would put her out of harm's way, at least for the moment.

She was a brave woman, one who led with her heart. He never thought he'd allow another woman into his life. But Lacy had slipped past his guard and forced him to confront the emptiness of his existence. She'd slipped into his arms and made him remember what it was like to need another human being. To love a woman.

Her blond hair was like the softest silk, and her kisses held the fire of banked passion that flared into life. Though he was the one accused of starting fires, it was Lacy who'd ignited the fire in his blood. She had brought him back to life after three years of living in a limbo of not feeling.

She had risked her future for him. She was his alibi, and he needed her. He'd long ago vowed never to put himself in a place where he needed another person. Now he needed Lacy, and instead of distress, he felt a surge of raw joy, because he knew he could count on her.

The sound of a limb snapping caught his attention. Rex, who'd been trotting silently beside him, stopped square in the trail. Hackles rising, the dog began to growl.

"Easy," Turner said softly. "Easy, Rex. We want him to come to us."

The dog settled slightly, but his alert gaze stayed focused on the woods to the left.

Turner followed the dog's lead and scanned the thicket of trees. He couldn't detect anything, but he trusted Rex's sense of smell and sight. Something or someone was out there.

"Come on, Rex," he said softly, nudging Buster forward. He had to pretend that he wasn't prepared for the attack, even as his hand slid into the pocket of his fleece jacket and found the small revolver.

Another noise from the left made him look in that direction just as Rex growled and sprang forward. He was completely unprepared for the blow that struck him on the right side of his head. Too late he realized that Buster had stumbled over some type of trip wire. Anthony had obviously been one step ahead of him— knowing he wouldn't go down the trail to Crossroads. The limb that struck him had come swinging out of the trees. His last thought before he hit the ground was that the trap had been cleverly conceived, and for all his care, he'd fallen right into it.

LACY SAW THE SMOKE before she rounded the last bend to the cabin. The smell of the fire was frightening, and she urged M&M into a gallop for the last several hundred yards of the trail. When she came into the clearing, the small cabin was already engulfed in flames.

There was no sign of Turner.

Heart in her throat, she slid off M&M and tied him to a tree a safe distance from the fire.

"Turner!" she called. "Turner!"

She ran toward the cabin. Was he inside? The fire was terrifically hot, but she rushed forward until she could kick the door. She managed to knock it open, but a tongue of flame leaped out at her, forcing her back.

"Turner!" she cried.

The heat drove her into the yard, and she watched helplessly as the old frame cabin burned. Sparks and hot ash spiraled up from the fire and were caught by the wind. Lacy watched in horror as they fell into the woods, smoldering in piles of old leaves and dried brush.

She ran to one small fire that had ignited and stomped it out. Nearby two more piles of dry brush burst into flame. She was able to extinguish them by stamping them out, but as she looked around, she realized that disaster was imminent. If a wildfire started and got away from her, the entire wilderness would go up in flames.

The summer had been dry, and the brief snowfall had done little to wet the parched earth. She saw another small fire and rushed over to kill it.

"I thought you were headed back to town. Turner used you as his alibi and now he's ready to get rid of you."

She whirled around to face Anthony. He was watching her with a cold smile.

"We have to keep the fire from spreading," Lacy said.

"Looks like you're going to be a busy lady for a little while. Your boyfriend got tired of burning structures and decided to do a *real* fire." He laughed.

"Where's Turner?" she asked.

"How would I know? I saw the smoke and came

to check it out. Looks like he's up to his old tricks, doesn't it?''

"He didn't do this." Lacy leaped to his defense before she even thought.

"I guess the place just caught on fire by itself. That's what Turner McLeod would like for you to believe." He said the words with anger. "I can see he charmed you just like he charmed my sister. Until the end. When she finally saw him for what he was, he had to kill her."

Lacy knew the note was still in the jacket pocket, and she knew that her faith in Turner had been strained. But not to the point that she could believe he'd killed a woman. It was one thing for her to doubt Turner, but quite another for Anthony to accuse him of being a cold-blooded killer.

"I don't know everything about Turner McLeod, but I can't believe he killed your sister."

"Well, it doesn't really matter what you believe," Anthony said conversationally. "Turner's going to confess. That's what's going to happen. And then he's going to prison, where he belongs. And you're going to help me put him there."

"I don't think so." Lacy turned and walked toward M&M. The horse was eyeing the blazing building nervously. "As soon as this fire is out, I'm going back down to talk to Sheriff Taylor." She untied M&M's reins to move him farther away from the fire. The wind had shifted and sparks were beginning to fall around the horse.

Anthony's hand on her shoulder was firm. "Don't be in such a rush," he said.

She shrugged him off. "Don't touch me again." Lacy led M&M to the corral. She left him tacked up, tying the reins over the saddle horn so there was no danger he might step on them. If she had to make a bolt for freedom, the gelding would be ready for her to leap into the saddle. The fire frightened her, but what she felt for Anthony was worse than fear. He wasn't the man who'd attacked her, but he was capable of violence. He was an angry bitter man.

"Why do you want to defend a man who would let you sacrifice everything for him? He's guilty, and yet he lets you defend him. Turner McLeod will pay for what he's done, but you're going to pay, too."

Lacy felt a stab of panic at Anthony's words. She swallowed the fear that rose in her throat.

"You have your doubts about him," Anthony said triumphantly. "If he confesses, then will you believe it?"

She hesitated. She had felt something so real with Turner, something that she'd never dreamed could really exist. Her heart told her that he was a good man, a decent man. Her brain told her that he had lied to her. The note was evidence of that. All her life she'd relied on her reasoning powers to survive. She'd sacrificed and scrimped and saved and planned, all to have a future as a writer. Yet something about Turner had motivated her to risk all that, because she believed in him.

Now her faith was shaky. But she knew this was a choice that would haunt her all the rest of her days.

"He won't confess, because he isn't guilty." She brushed past Anthony and stamped out another fire. "Look, over there." She pointed to another small flame licking hungrily at a dead cedar tree. "Help me," she said. "Any of these small fires could get away from us."

Anthony didn't move. "I didn't come here to help you save Turner. I came here to make sure he got what he deserved."

"Turner isn't guilty, but if he is, why can't you let the law handle it?" she asked.

"I tried that. He bought his way out of it."

Lacy grabbed a pail and went to the hand pump. She filled the pail and rushed over to the burning cedar. As she drenched the tree, there was a loud satisfying sizzle.

Ignoring Anthony, Lacy checked the burning cabin. The old timber had gone up like a torch, and at last the flames were beginning to die down. Perhaps the worst was over. Eventually Turner would return and she would ask him about the note. Anthony had not intended to bolster her support of Turner, but that was exactly what had happened.

"If you aren't going to help me contain the fire, would you please leave?" Lacy asked him. She was afraid of him, afraid of the emotion she saw deep in his brown eyes. The last thing she wanted, though, was for him to know it.

"You have a chance to save yourself," he said.

"If I feel in need of rescue, I'll keep you in mind," she said.

The sarcasm was a mistake. Anthony stepped closer to her, his mouth a hard line of fury. "Lonnie said you'd come along willingly. He said you were smarter than Lilith. But you're not. You're just like her. He's got you fooled, and you're going to end up dead if I don't do something."

"I don't think Lonnie is giving very good advice," Lacy said, knowing that her only hope was to brave it out. ''Lonnie must be the man you were with before—the trapper, right?''

Anthony's arms went around her so suddenly that Lacy didn't know what to do at first. When she realized that he intended to restrain her, she lashed out with her booted foot. The first blow was lucky and she caught him directly on the shin.

He gave a yelp and released her. As he hopped on one leg, she took aim and kicked him twice as hard in the other shin. Anthony went down like a sack of potatoes. Lacy wasted no time running to the corral where M&M was waiting. She knew he could jump the fence, so she didn't bother dropping the gate poles to the ground. She ducked through the fence, jumped on his back and kicked him into a gallop.

She'd never jumped in her life. She leaned down, grabbed the saddle horn and closed her eyes as she felt M&M's athletic body lift over the fence. In the space of a second she felt his front feet touch and then his back. They were over the fence! They were on their way.

She opened her eyes and found Anthony directly in M&M's path. The horse balked and reared, trying to avoid running the man down. Lacy felt a fearful moment of déjà vu.

''Go, M!'' she urged the horse. The Appaloosa made to move forward again, but not before Anthony grabbed her leg.

''Don't make me pull you off that horse,'' he said through gritted teeth as he reached up and clasped her waist.

''Was it your friend who pulled me off the horse and smacked me the last time?'' Lacy asked angrily. She used her elbow to try to break his grip on her.

"I don't know what you're talking about, but you aren't going anywhere. This is for your own safety. Turner McLeod is eventually going to kill you, and I'm not going to let that happen."

Anthony gave a mighty tug, and Lacy felt her grip on the saddle loosen. Tightening her legs, she realized she was off balance. She made one final grasp at the saddle horn. For a split second she was able to hang on to the saddle, but Anthony's superior strength overpowered her. She felt her body slipping from the saddle, and M&M moved out from under her.

As the gelding charged away, she fell onto the hard rocky ground. Anthony hauled her to her feet.

"You're coming with me," he said. "Turner McLeod is going to confess, and you're going to help me get the confession out of him."

Lacy started to resist, but it was pointless. Anthony scooped her up and began to head back into the wilderness with her.

Struggle and fight as she might, she couldn't shake free of him. When he finally set her on her feet and looked down at her, she had never been so afraid.

"I suggest that you walk ahead of me without any more trouble. If you don't, I'll have to drag you. I can do that, but it won't be pleasant. For either of us."

Lacy looked back at the burning cabin. "I can't leave the fire," she said. Although the blaze was subduing, ashes and embers spiraled up in the flames. The wind was still catching them and blowing them into the woods, where they had the possibility of igniting small fires.

"Turner set the fire—he can worry about it," Anthony said. He looked up at the sun, which was beginning to lower into the western horizon. "We don't have time to wait." He gave Lacy a push. "Start moving, and don't try anything stupid," he said.

"Kidnapping is a more serious offense than arson," Lacy said.

"This isn't kidnapping. This is a rescue," Anthony said. "When you learn the truth, you'll appreciate the effort Lonnie and I have gone to to save you."

Lacy didn't answer. She glanced over her shoulder and thought her heart would stop. A small tree beside the cabin was burning brightly.

"Anthony!" She pointed back toward the cabin.

He turned and looked and a slow grin spread over his face. "Turner's going to be in serious trouble," he said with satisfaction. "This time he's started a fire that's going to burn him bad."

"We can stop it," Lacy said, starting to push past him. "We still have time to stop it."

He caught her arm. "You can walk or I can drag you, which is it going to be?"

Lacy tried to ignore him. She jerked free. "We can't let the woods catch fire!" she said with exasperation.

"Oh, yes, we can, and that's exactly what we're going to do." He pulled a nylon cord out of his jacket pocket and caught her wrists. Even though she fought him, he tied her hands together. Using the end of the cord as a tether, he continued to move away from the cabin.

Lacy pulled against the tether, but Anthony jerked hard enough to make her fall to her knees. The sharp rocks reinjured the wounds she'd sustained earlier.

She cried out in pain, but Anthony kept walking. She was forced to stand up and follow or else be dragged.

The last thing she saw as she glanced back at the cabin was the small tree, now burning brightly, an orange glow in the fading day.

Chapter Sixteen

Turner awoke to the smell of fire and a view of rocky ground. It took several moments for his head to clear enough for him to realize he was hanging over the saddle on Buster.

Rex stood on his hind legs and licked Turner's face, whining softly in his throat. Turner was glad the dog was concerned—he was worried, too.

Buster began to shift and dance again, and Turner knew that something was very wrong. Though he tried to wriggle off the horse, he couldn't budge. He was tied across the saddle.

And his head felt as if a sledgehammer had been wielded against it.

Snorting, Buster began to hop. "Come on, old fella," Turner soothed the horse as he tried to figure out what to do. He could smell the fire. The woods were burning. And Buster was obviously tied in such a manner that he couldn't get free, either.

Turner went over what he could remember. He'd been riding when he'd heard a noise in one direction, and then he'd been struck in the head by a limb from the other direction. It had been a very crafty trap.

Was it possible that now someone had left him tied up to burn to death with his horse?

Lacy! Worry about his own predicament completely evaporated as he thought about her. What had happened to her?

"Rex, you have to find Lacy," he said. "You have to bring her here."

The crackling of the fire was growing louder, and Turner couldn't be certain if it was his imagination or not, but he thought he felt a warm breath of wind. It was as if the flames were being slowly pushed in his direction.

Buster backed up and began to pull furiously at the log he was tied to. Turner knew then that he wasn't imagining anything. The fire was creeping steadily toward them.

He swiveled his head and saw that Rex was still waiting.

"Go find Lacy," he ordered.

Instead of trotting off, Rex only whined. Turner accepted that it was pointless. Rex wasn't going to leave him. He'd have to figure out how to get off the horse, untie himself and get them all to safety, then he found Lacy.

As he twisted his hands, he realized he'd been tied with some kind of nylon rope. It was thin and had been pulled tight, but he concentrated on stretching the rope. Nylon had a certain amount of give, and if he could simply get a tad of slack, he'd figure out a way to slip free.

Even as he worked with the bonds, he caught another strong whiff of the fire, and a large black ash floated in and settled on the ground by Buster's hoof.

There wasn't time to waste. Turner called Rex over

to him. He struggled to get his hands as close to the dog as he could. "Now's your chance," he said, wondering if the puppy he'd discouraged from chewing would ever understand.

Rex sniffed the bonds, then very gently began to gnaw on them. Turner heaved a sigh of thanks as he waited for Rex's sharp canines to do the job.

It took better than five minutes, but Turner shook off the ropes and then untied the loop that held him to the saddle. In a few moments he was on his feet. Buster was still pulling on the rope that held him and rolling his eyes until the whites showed.

"No time now for hysterics," he said to the horse as he untied him. "We have to find Lacy and make sure she's out of the way of the fire."

It seemed that freedom was all Buster wanted. As soon as Turner swung back into the saddle, the horse set off at a trot. It was only when Turner changed directions and started back toward the cabin that Buster balked. The horse refused to head toward the fire.

Turner allowed the horse to stand for a moment. He spoke reassuringly and stroked Buster's neck and shoulder. All animals were terrified of fire. Their instincts were to run from it. Buster was only acting in self-preservation.

Turner knew that he was going to have to convince the horse to act against his instincts. He wondered if he wasn't making a foolish mistake by going back toward the cabin. Yet he had to go.

Nudging Buster with his legs, he coaxed the horse forward. With each yard he went deeper into the woods, the more he realized that the fire he was headed toward was big and hot and very dangerous.

If he'd had any ideas that he might be able to put it out, he accepted that he needed professional help. He could only hope that the fire rangers were alert.

Picking his way carefully around the edge of the fire, he felt sick. The wilderness he loved was in danger. And Lacy was on the other side of that fire. He had to make sure she was okay.

Although Buster kept shying sideways, Turner pushed him forward. At last the horse responded, and Turner knew that the animal had fought his fear and fallen back on trust.

Urging the horse into a gallop, Turner flew over the uneven ground with Rex beside him. Dusk had fallen by the time he got to the clearing where the cabin had once stood. All that was left were burning embers that glowed a hot orange against the rapidly dwindling daylight.

Turner saw no sign of Lacy, but it didn't take him long to figure out that the fire had started at the cabin. Someone had torched the cabin, and then hot ashes had blown into the dry woods. He followed the tracks of the fire with dismay.

If firefighters came now, the blaze could be contained. But in another few hours, it would be burning so hot that the least amount of wind could make it one of the worst disasters to hit the wilderness in decades.

His only consolation was that there was no sign of Lacy. She'd gone in the opposite direction, and if she'd followed his plan, she was safely down the trail away from the fire. He took a deep breath. There was that to be thankful for.

Beneath him Buster tensed, and Turner prepared for the horse to jump forward. Normally Buster was the calmest mount anyone could ever want, but the fire had so rattled the gelding that he was nervous about everything.

When the big Appaloosa came rushing at them out of the brush, Turner's heart sank. Easing over to M&M, Turner gathered the reins. If M&M was here, where was Lacy? He knew that no matter what answer he came up with, it wasn't good. Lacy was in trouble.

He whistled Rex to his side and reached into his pocket. When he'd traded jackets with Lacy, he'd found one of her kerchiefs tucked in the pocket. He'd taken it and put it in his own pocket. It had been a sentimental thing to do, but now he realized the worth of it. He held it down to Rex's nose.

"Find her, boy."

Where Rex had refused to abandon Turner when he was tied to the horse, the shepherd put his nose immediately to the ground and began sniffing in a circle. When he picked up the trail, he looked up at Turner and barked.

"Find her," Turner repeated. "Hurry."

Rex took off like he'd been shot from a cannon, and to Turner's relief, he headed away from the flames.

LACY FELT AS IF HER LEGS were going to buckle under her. She and Anthony had been walking for two hours. Darkness had fallen and she could no longer see the trail. They'd left the fire behind, but Lacy couldn't shake the images that popped in her head of small creatures fleeing the horror of the flames.

She had no idea where she was going or what Anthony intended to do with her. Worry for Turner gnawed at her.

"I'm tired," she said, sitting on a stump. "I can't go any farther. I need water."

Anthony pulled a canteen from around his shoulder and handed it to her. "We're almost there. You'll get food and rest when we arrive."

Lacy wasn't so sure about that. Since she'd given up most resistance, Anthony had been uncommunicative. He'd also stopped tugging on the tether that still was tied to her hands.

"I have to go to the bathroom," she said.

He looked at her. "Wait."

"I can't." She knew it was the one chance she'd have to get her hands free.

"If you try to run," he said, "I'll catch you." He untied her and nodded at the direction he wanted her to take.

Lacy rubbed her wrists. The freedom to dangle her arms at her sides was a pleasure she'd taken for granted all her life. She stumbled into the darkness wondering how she could best use this opportunity.

If help was on the way, it might behoove her to try to escape. Surely the rangers had seen the fire. If she could head back that way, she might run into a rescue party.

There was also the chance that the Brisco County sheriff had sent someone to try to find Turner.

"Hurry up," Anthony called out to her. "Lonnie's going to be waiting for us. And he doesn't like to be kept waiting."

"Great," she said under her breath. She sneaked deeper into the woods. The night was overcast, and though she couldn't see two feet in front of her face, she knew that Anthony suffered from the same disadvantage.

She was about to make a break for freedom when the beam of a flashlight blinded her. She threw up both hands.

"Looks like you're finished," Anthony said. "Now let's get moving. If you don't try to run, I won't tie your hands again."

Lacy walked back to the trail, which she could barely make out in the glare of the flashlight. She hadn't acted fast enough. Escape had been denied her.

"Why are you doing this?" she asked Anthony. She made her voice sound reasonable.

"You're in danger with that man."

"I don't think that's true."

He pushed her slightly, forcing her to keep walking.

"Turner isn't the man you think he is," she said. She had to somehow convince Anthony of that—or at least make him believe that justice would be done if Turner were guilty. "He told me about the other fires. He swears he wasn't involved."

"He can swear all day and all night. I don't believe him," Anthony replied. "Keep walking."

"Why would he do such a thing?"

"Lilith rejected him. He couldn't stand it. Since he couldn't have her, he killed her."

Lacy thought for a moment before she answered. "That doesn't make sense, Anthony. Turner left. He was getting on with his life." She took a breath. "I talked to Toby Dodds, the sheriff in your town. He doesn't believe Turner is guilty. In fact, he gave us a chance to come back to Brisco County and prove that

Turner was with me when the sheriff's house caught fire."

In the darkness she couldn't tell what impact her words were having on Anthony. She could only keep trying.

"There were fires before Lilith. You know that Turner's brother, Benjamin, died in a fire." She waited, but there was no response. She kept moving forward as slowly as she dared. "He loved his brother. There was no reason for him to want to hurt his family."

"Maybe he's just mean. Maybe when he doesn't get what he wants, he burns something."

"I don't believe that, and I don't think you can know such a thing. I can't help wondering why you're so determined to believe that Turner hurt your sister. The fire was ruled an accident." Her hand went unconsciously to the note still in the pocket of the jacket. It was a real risk, but Lacy knew she didn't have a lot of cards to play, or a lot of time.

"Keep walking and quit talking," Anthony said. "We'll be where we're going shortly."

"I have a note that your sister wrote," she said carefully. "Where did it come from? Do you know?"

"Lilith wrote it. She wrote it just before she died."

"How do you know that?" Lacy asked. "Did she give it to you?"

There was a silence. "I found it."

"Her house burned to the ground. Where did you find it?" Lacy pressed.

"She left it for me."

"She left it for you—or for Turner?" Lacy wasn't sure what she was after, but something was very wrong here.

"She left it for him."

Lacy bit her lip. "Turner had left town. Lilith knew that. He honored her request and left town immediately. He was in LaFayette."

"That's what he says."

"That's the truth," Lacy said. "Sheriff Dodds believed Turner. So did the newspaper editor."

"Turner must have given them a lot of cash."

"There's not enough money in the world for Lilith's killer to buy his way out of her death. In case you weren't aware, everyone in town loved your sister."

"Just shut up. Shut up and keep moving."

There was anger in Anthony's voice, but also some confusion. Lacy wasn't ready to give up yet. "Who gave you that note, Anthony? Think about that."

Lacy decided the best thing to do was bide her time for the moment. She'd given Anthony something to think about.

TURNER KEPT RIDING. In the darkness he had to let Buster have his head, and he was ponying M&M beside him. Every so often, he called Rex back to him to be sure he was following the dog.

The route led into the wilderness. In the several weeks Turner had been in the area, he'd scouted around and discovered a couple more abandoned cabins, all in worse shape than the one he'd claimed for his own.

That had to be where Lacy was heading. But since she didn't know the area, she must have been captured and was being led by someone. And Turner had a pretty good idea of who that someone was. Anthony. His plan to lure Anthony had clearly backfired.

He was heartsick over the fire. The wind had at
least died down, so when the firefighters arrived,
they'd stand a better chance of containing the blaze
and extinguishing it. Had his concern for Lacy not
been so great, he would have remained behind to help
fight the blaze.

Regret gnawed at him. He should have turned himself in as Lacy had suggested. She would be safe now
and there would have been no blaze.

Anthony was behind the fire—that was the only
conclusion he could draw. Anthony had set the sheriff's house on fire, and then the cabin. But had he
burned his own sister's house? If the answer to that
was yes, then he was dealing with a man even more
disturbed than he'd first realized.

Lacy was in grave danger.

He urged Buster to walk faster. He considered tying
the horses and walking, but if Lacy was injured, she
might need a mount. The best he could do was keep
moving in the darkness and hope he found Lacy before she was hurt.

LACY REMAINED SILENT as long as she could.
"Why'd you burn Turner's cabin?" she asked.

There was a snort. "I didn't set that fire. Your
friend Turner started it. He's the one who sets all the
fires."

"Turner's research was in the cabin. He wouldn't
have burned all that up."

"He doesn't care about anything. The sooner you
realize that, the better off you're going to be," Anthony said. "Now be quiet. We're almost there."

Even as he spoke, Lacy stepped from the trees into
a clearing. The small cabin was so dark that she al-

most missed it in the blackness of the night. When she saw the dwelling, her heart sank. Once she was inside, her chances of escape would be even smaller than they were outside.

As if Anthony had read her mind, he grabbed her shoulder. "Don't try anything dumb. Lonnie's here, and he doesn't have a lot of patience."

"What's all this to Lonnie?" Lacy asked. "Why is he involved?"

"He and Lilith were friends," Anthony said. "We were all friends, until Turner came along." Pushing her up onto the small porch, he called, "Lonnie! We're here! Open up."

Lacy held her breath, remembering the cold eyes of the second man. When there was no answer, she felt a slight relief. Anthony was a dangerous man, but he didn't seem completely cold-blooded.

"I won't tell the sheriff about any of this if you'll just let me go," she said. "We have to get help for the fire."

"Too late for that. Either help has come or it's too late. We're just lucky we're upwind of it."

"You can't be that hard!" Lacy exclaimed, losing her patience. "Thousands of acres might burn."

"That's just more evidence against Turner."

She sighed and stepped inside the cabin, then stopped. It was so dark she couldn't see a thing. She felt Anthony brush by her as he stepped farther into the room.

It was probably the only chance she was going to get. She rushed back out the door as fast as she could. She let her memory work as she bounded across the rickety porch and leaped to the ground. It was so dark she could barely make out the biggest trees, but she didn't slow. If she could only get a short distance away, she could hide.

Until...what?

Until daybreak or until she could figure out a better plan. All she knew was that she had no desire to remain in the cabin with Anthony and his friend Lonnie, who'd doubtless show up any minute.

A tree limb caught her across the chest and the breath whooshed out of her lungs. When she fell to her knees, she continued scrambling.

"Hey! Come back here!"

She heard Anthony thudding after her. She could tell when he hit the dirt beside the cabin. He was only yards behind her.

Still on her hands and knees, she ducked behind a tree and tried to suck air into her lungs without making any noise. She was terrified and her pulse pounded in her ears.

There was the glow of a lamp inside the cabin, and Lacy was able at last to get her bearings. At least now she knew what direction to move away from the two men. She had her wind back and she slowly crawled deeper into the woods. All she had to do was keep moving. She was tired and freezing and hungry and thirsty, but none of that mattered. She had ten hours of darkness to survive, and in the morning she'd find help. All she had to do was keep moving deeper into the woods.

The sound of a door slamming stopped her. She pressed herself deep into the fronds of a cedar tree and listened.

"Where the hell is the girl?" Lonnie asked. She recognized his voice.

"She got away," Anthony confessed.

"You're a fool!" Lonnie shouted. "You had the easy job, and you let a girl make a fool of you."

"She's around here," Lonnie said. "She couldn't get far. I was lighting the lamp and she ran out the door. She's only been gone a few minutes."

"Give me the flashlight."

She dared a peek through the trees and saw the two men silhouetted on the porch of the cabin. One of them had a high-beamed flashlight and was shining it through the woods. When it swung her way, she instinctively shrank back against the trunk of the tree.

"We'll get her," Anthony said. "We'll get her and then we'll make Turner McLeod pay."

"He's already paid," Lonnie said as he jumped off the porch. "He paid just the way Lilith did."

"What do you mean?" Anthony asked. "We have to get him to confess."

"It's too late for that. Now let's find that girl and make sure she doesn't talk to anyone."

Fear for Turner almost paralyzed her, but she forced herself to start crawling away from the cabin. She moved as fast as she could without making any noise. Rocks and sticks stabbed at her palms and knees, but she kept going. The dense foliage and tree trunks confused her sense of direction. Her own breath seemed to roar in her ears.

She felt something round beneath her hand and stopped. She felt it slowly, recognizing the smooth leather of a boot. Attached to it was denim. Very slowly she looked up the pair of legs and into darkness. When the flashlight beam blinked on and blinded her, she didn't need to see that it was Lonnie who'd tracked her down.

She knew it was him by his laugh.

"It's okay, Anthony," Lonnie called out as he grabbed her hair and lifted her to her feet. "I've got her. And she won't be getting away from us again."

Chapter Seventeen

Turner knew the cabin was nearby. The fire was far enough behind them that Buster and M&M were completely calm, so when he dismounted, he dropped the reins to the ground. The horses were trained to "ground tie"—to remain standing where they were without actually being tied—and would wait for his return.

With Rex at his side, he eased slowly through the trees. Beside him, Rex gave a whine that ended on a low growl.

He put a hand on the dog's neck to keep him still. There was no point rushing into a situation until he knew what was happening.

He saw the dim light of the lantern in the cabin. He'd looked at this place as a possibility for his own headquarters, but it was in worse shape than the cabin he'd chosen. At one time someone had homesteaded the area, but the rocky soil and dry conditions had driven the homesteaders to gentler land.

Several windows in the cabin had been boarded up, but he eased around the perimeter until he came to one that still had glass. Looking inside, he saw the two men and Lacy. She was sitting in a chair with her hands tied behind her back and her mouth gagged. The sight of it infuriated him, but he knew that he had only one chance to save her. He couldn't allow his anger to rule him. He had to think clearly and carefully. He had to find out what Anthony and Lonnie were planning. Moving as close to the cabin as he dared, Turner strained to listen. The voices were muffled, but he could make them out.

"You said if I got the girl, Turner would follow and we could make him confess," Anthony said. He was extremely upset.

"It didn't work out that way," Lonnie answered. "I told him you had the girl, and he said that was too bad for her. He started to ride away, so I had to do something."

"I wanted his confession to Lilith's murder," Anthony said. "You said you'd make him tell the truth."

Turner chanced a longer look inside. Lacy was shaking her head and thudding her feet on the floor. Anthony scowled at her. "She's about as stubborn as a mule," he said. "The whole way up here she tried to convince me Turner was innocent." There was a pause. "She asked about the note from Lilith."

"Come on outside on the porch," Lonnie said. "We need to square away the last of the details." He looked meaningfully at Lacy.

Lacy thumped the floor with all of her might, but the two men started toward the door.

Turner eased back into the darkness of the night. He couldn't risk being seen by the men. Somewhere along the way he'd lost the small pistol he'd bought. Either the man who'd attacked him had taken it, or it had fallen out of his pocket. He had no weapon, only his wits.

LACY TWISTED AT THE ROPES that held her hands. Lonnie had shown no mercy once he'd captured her. He'd tied her in the chair, gagged her and then pretended she was a piece of furniture. Even though she couldn't talk, she could hear. And she was very worried. What had they done to Turner? Lonnie sounded as if Turner was dead. The idea made her feel sick to her stomach, and she couldn't risk that, not wearing a gag. Instead, she thought about the note from Lilith.

Where had it come from? If Lilith had burned, along with all her belongings, who had the note? Why hadn't it been given to the sheriff? The more she thought about it, the more frightened she became.

Whoever had the note had seen Lilith before she died. The obvious person was Anthony, her brother. But Lacy knew that wasn't the case. Someone had given Anthony the note, and she was willing to bet that someone was Lonnie.

She remembered Anthony's words. They had all been friends until Turner arrived. Lilith and Lonnie and Anthony. She also remembered what the sheriff had said about Lilith. She'd been a popular girl, a beautiful girl who attracted more than her share of interested men.

Some of them had been hard to discourage.

Lacy tugged at her bonds. She had to get free and she had to talk to Anthony. Lonnie wasn't the secondary man in this scheme, he was the mastermind. He'd manipulated Anthony. She wasn't certain of his motives, but she believed he was behind the fire at Lilith's house, the fire at Sheriff Taylor's house and the burning of the cabin. She knew it as well as she knew her name.

Somehow she had to convince Anthony that he was

being used. While Anthony wanted Turner's confession, she had the feeling that Lonnie wanted something a lot more deadly.

Tugging at the ropes, she tried to listen for the two men. They had gone outside, but they weren't far. She was their prize, and she knew exactly what her role was going to be. She was the goat tied to the stake to attract the tiger.

She heard laughter from the porch and resumed her struggle against her bonds.

Anthony came back inside. He was alone. Now was her chance. She made a choking sound, as if the gag had begun to suffocate her.

"No more tricks," he said as he pulled the tape free. "Lonnie said if you gave us any more trouble, he'd fix you so you couldn't."

"No trouble," she said, drawing in a full deep breath. "Anthony, listen to me. Lonnie is the one who killed Lilith. He's—"

"Hush up!" he snapped. "If you don't, I'll put the tape back over your mouth."

"Think about it," she said. "Lonnie's the one who gave you the note from Lilith, isn't he? Where did he get it? Where?" And the final trump. "Why didn't he bring Turner here to defend himself? Maybe it was because he couldn't risk you finding out the truth, Anthony."

She saw the doubt cross his face. "That note should have burned in the house with your sister. If Lilith wrote it, she would have had it in her house, ready to send to Turner. But she didn't know where Turner had gone. He left without telling a single person where he was going because he didn't know himself. So why would she have even written it? And if she did write it, why did Lonnie have it?''

"She wrote it because she was hurt. Turner betrayed her. She wrote it—''

"She wrote it because Lonnie made her write it. He made her write it before he knocked her out and set fire to the house.'' Lacy knew she'd stumbled on the truth, and the danger of her situation, and that of Turner and Anthony, almost paralyzed her with fear. But she couldn't give in. She had to keep talking, had to make Anthony see what had suddenly become very very clear to her.

"That's not true!'' Anthony said hotly. "Lonnie loved her. He wanted to marry her, and he would have, except Turner came along and stole her from him.''

Lacy leaned as close to Anthony as her bonds would allow. "No one can steal another person's love. Turner didn't take anything from Lonnie. Lilith gave Turner her love. She gave it to him. Not Lonnie. Can't you see that?''

She saw that he did see it, and that the horror of it was almost more than he could bear.

"No,'' he whispered. "Lonnie wouldn't do that. He was my friend, and he loved Lilith.''

"And Lilith loved Turner. Maybe Lonnie didn't intend to kill her. Maybe he only meant to frighten her and to frame Turner for burning the house. But she didn't get out of the house. She died there, Anthony, and it was because of your friend.''

The thoughts that flickered through Anthony's mind weren't hard to read. His rugged features clearly showed the doubt, then confusion that he felt. Lacy had to drive home the truth to him—to make him see once and for all that Lonnie was the man who deserved punishment, not Turner.

"Who set the fire at the sheriff's house?" she pressed. "It was Lonnie, wasn't it. He did it to frame Turner. Just like he burned the cabin. Can't you see that he's the one who's been setting the fires all along?" Anger began to replace the confusion on Anthony's face. She had convinced him, or at least she'd given him room to doubt Turner's absolute guilt. She leaned closer and whispered in his ear, "You know what I'm saying is true. Help me find out what Lonnie did to Turner before it's too late."

"I don't know," he said, leaning back suddenly.

Lacy looked up and felt her heart leap into her throat. Lonnie was standing in the doorway holding the gun that Turner had bought from Melton Weeks at the supply store.

"What's going on here?" Lonnie asked, his gaze shifting from Anthony to Lacy.

"You were right about her," Anthony said as he stood up. With a quick fluid gesture he pressed the tape back over Lacy's mouth. "She pretended to be choking, and when I took off the tape, she started right in on how innocent poor Turner is." He chuckled. "She's kind of cute in the way she goes about it."

Lonnie lowered the gun so that it hung casually at his side, but his gaze pinned Anthony. "I told you not to let her talk."

"No harm done," Anthony said easily. "Nothing she says is going to change the fact that my sister is dead." He shrugged. "I thought she was choking to death."

"Now we wouldn't want to let that happen." Lonnie seemed to visibly relax. He went to the door and stared into the darkness. "It shouldn't be long now. I'll bet the firefighters are already on the ground. We ought to be on our way, which means we need to take care of one final bit of business," he said.

"What do you mean?" Anthony asked.

Lacy knew that Lonnie wasn't referring to Turner's confession, because Lonnie knew that Turner was innocent and would eventually prove it. No. Lonnie didn't intend to let Turner leave the wilderness alive. Or her, either.

"I want to ask the little lady a few questions," Lonnie said. He went to the corner and picked up a hunting rifle that looked state-of-the-art to Lacy. The weapon was sleek and modern and had a big scope on it. He held the weapon out to Anthony. "Go on out and make sure we're all alone up here."

Anthony hesitated.

"What's wrong?" Lonnie asked sharply.

Anthony took the gun. "Nothing. You're not going to hurt her, are you?"

"Who's in charge of the details?" Lonnie asked. "Who's in charge of the plan?"

"You are," Anthony said innocently.

"Then do what you're told." Lonnie walked behind Lacy and put his hands on her shoulders. "You should do what you're told, Anthony. I know how much it distresses you when a woman's unhappy."

Lacy didn't allow herself to move, even when he tightened his grip on her shoulders. He wasn't hurting her, but he was sending a clear message. To her and Anthony. And Anthony understood. He understood everything.

"I'll go take a look," he said agreeably. "I'll be back soon."

"Be careful," Lonnie warned.

TURNER WAS READY when the cabin door opened and Anthony stepped out onto the porch. He'd been waiting in the woods, hoping for just such an opportunity, one that would allow him to tackle the men individually.

Turner angled through the trees so that he could come at Anthony from the side. In the darkness he couldn't clearly see the weapon Anthony carried, but he knew it was a rifle of some type. Turner had only his hands.

When he was at an angle facing Anthony's right shoulder, he started moving forward as carefully as he could. He needed the last second of surprise.

He started running and launched himself at Anthony, hitting him just below the shoulder. He struck with such force that Anthony was pushed off the porch and propelled away from the cabin. They hit the dirt and continued to roll into the yard.

Turner found himself straddling the younger man, his fist drawn back in preparation. Rex was at his side. The dog snared Anthony's wrist and held it firmly in his jaws. A low growl warned Anthony not to try anything.

"You didn't kill Lilith," Anthony said.

Turner was so shocked that he sat back, his fist still drawn. "What?"

"I know you didn't kill my sister." Anthony's lips compressed into a bitter smile. "All along it was Lonnie. He killed Lilith and set every other fire that's been set. We were trying to frame you, and we're guilty of the awful things we blamed you for.''

"Why did he kill Lilith?'' Turner asked, pushing to his feet and offering a hand to help Anthony up. As soon as Turner relaxed, Rex let go of Anthony and stepped back.

"He loved her, and when she fell in love with you, he couldn't stand it. Oh, he pretended that he was still her friend, that he understood. But he didn't. He hated you.''

"But to kill her?'' Turner was still shocked.

"I don't believe he wanted to kill her.'' Anthony took a deep breath. "As horrible as it sounds, I think he only wanted to make her hate you. If he could frame you as an arsonist and attempted murderer, then Lilith would get over you. Whatever he intended, Lilith died.''

Turner was stunned by the sudden turn of events, but he was quickly beginning to come to a terrifying conclusion. Lacy was in the cabin with a man who'd already killed one young woman. Would Lonnie view Lacy as another female victim of Turner's? And if he did, what would he do?

"We have to get Lacy out of there,'' Turner said.

"I've been trying to figure out how. We have to do something fast. Lonnie thinks you're dead, and that woman in there is just a loose end to him.''

There was movement in the cabin and Turner dashed into the nearby trees. Anthony sat up slowly.

"What's going on out here?'' Lonnie asked.

Anthony gave a sheepish chuckle. "I sort of tripped on a root.'' He bent down and picked up the rifle. "I'm okay.''

Lonnie remained in the doorway. "Be careful,'' he

said slowly. "It's mighty easy for a person to get hurt out in the wilderness. Even a minor scrape can be serious."

The door closed.

Turner felt his heart rate increase. Lonnie knew something was wrong. He suspected that Anthony's loyalty had changed—it was clear in the way he spoke to him.

Turner had learned one big lesson about the wilderness. A trapped animal is always the most dangerous. Lonnie was trapped, but he had the advantage of holding Lacy as his hostage.

LACY KNEW SOMETHING was wrong the moment Lonnie came back inside after checking on Anthony. She saw it in his eyes, in the way he looked at her as he slowly closed the door and softly slid the thumb bolt home.

Anthony was locked out.

He kept his eyes on her as he moved slowly toward her, obviously relishing the fact that he frightened her, though Lacy did all she could to hide her fear.

"Things have changed," he said softly, tearing off the tape so brutally that Lacy thought her skin might have gone with it.

"You're a real bastard." She put her lips together for a moment to ease the stinging. "Anthony knows the truth. He knows you killed Lilith." She intended to shock him and she'd succeeded. "You might as well give it up."

"He'll never believe I killed his sister. Anthony loved Lilith so much that he wanted someone to blame for her death. He's been mighty helpful to me in setting Turner up for a big fall. Two murders and a host of fires.'' He chuckled softly, almost to himself.

''Anthony doesn't believe you anymore,'' Lacy insisted. ''Call him in here and ask him.'' She smiled. ''You locked the door because you know what I'm saying is true.''

''I have the trump, though,'' he said with a cruel smile. ''I have you. Turner is dead. Anthony may not believe what I tell him anymore, but he's in this as deep as I am. He can't back out now.''

Lacy tried to control her racing heart, the taste of fear that threatened to make her gag. ''What did Turner ever do to make you hate him so much?'' Lacy asked.

''His father destroyed my family. My dad lost his business and then he shot himself. He was so ashamed. He died thinking he was a failure, and it was all because of those damn McLeods.''

''But Turner wasn't...'' And then Lacy understood. ''You set fire to the McLeod home. You killed Turner's brother.''

''Nobody was supposed to die. I just wanted to show them what it felt like to lose everything you cared about. When my father died, we lost our home, everything. The McLeods just got insurance money and built another house. Turner went on to college. He never suffered, so I decided that he should.''

''Why did you kill Lilith?'' Lacy asked.

''I only meant to scare her,'' Lonnie said. He shook his head. ''I gave her some sleeping pills and I was going to make sure she woke up and got out. But the fire got too hot too fast. There wasn't anything I could do, and she didn't wake up.''

"How'd you get the note?" Lacy asked. It was one of the last things she needed answered.

"I made her write it. I was going to give it to the sheriff and make Lilith say it was true. She was afraid I'd hurt Turner. That's why she told him she didn't love him. That's how much she loved me. She broke her engagement to Turner and sent him away because she thought he wasn't safe. Then she knew that the two of us could be together."

Lacy nodded as if she understood, but the insanity of Lonnie's reasoning only served to frighten her more thoroughly. She heard what he was saying, and in her mind's eye she saw poor Lilith writing such a strange and unusual note. She'd been coerced. And then she'd been killed.

Lacy was unprepared for the hand in her hair that tugged her head back. "I wish I could shoot you, but Turner's method of killing is fire. I guess you'll have to burn." Lonnie released her hair and picked up a five-gallon container of kerosene. Without another word, he started to pour the liquid on the floor of the cabin.

Suddenly splinters of wood flew everywhere as the door was kicked off its hinges. Turner and Anthony came flying into the room, rolling and coming up on their feet like trained law officers. Right behind them was Rex. The dog flew past Turner and thudded into Lonnie's chest, sending the kerosene container and the pistol he held tumbling across the floor.

Lacy shifted her knees out of the way as Turner connected an uppercut to Lonnie's jaw. The blow was so hard it knocked the man across the room. He fell back into the old stove where a low fire burned.

Lonnie yelled and jumped up, the seat of his pants burning. Tiny flames began to move up his shirt.

"Outside!" Turner ordered, grabbing him and propelling him out the door, where Turner threw him to the ground and began to roll him in the dirt to extinguish the flames.

Anthony knelt beside her, untying the ropes.

"I'm sorry," he said. "I really believed that Turner had killed my sister. I've done some terrible things. I don't know what to say."

"I'm not hurt," Lacy told him. "Turner is the person you've damaged. He's the one you need to talk to."

"I will," Anthony promised. "As soon as we get back to Claytonville, I'll tell the sheriff everything."

Chapter Eighteen

About half a mile from Turner's old burned cabin, Lacy spotted the firefighters. They looked exhausted, but their efforts had been successful. The blaze had consumed better than a thousand acres, but it was under control.

Sitting on M&M's back, Lacy was delighted to see Brisco County Sheriff Paul Taylor. He was seated on the ground among several firefighters and Brisco County volunteers, who'd helped fight the blaze.

Lacy twisted around to see Turner, who was behind her leading Buster with Lonnie on his back. Lonnie's hands were tied to the saddle horn. Anthony walked beside Turner, and they had talked quietly during the long walk.

Rex had darted in and out of the small entourage, and he bounded up to Lacy's side protectively as several of the worn-out firefighters sighted them and began to rise.

Sheriff Taylor was stumbling with fatigue, but when he saw Turner, he regained his vitality. Hand on the butt of his gun, he came toward them. "You're under arrest," he said. "You have the right—"

"Turner didn't set your house on fire, Sheriff. Lonnie and I did it,'' Anthony said. He ignored the glare that Lonnie shot him. ''It's a long story. Turner didn't start any of the fires.''

The sheriff looked from one to the other, weighing what might be happening among the bedraggled group. He settled on Lacy.

''What's this all about?'' he asked her.

She was almost too exhausted to speak, but she gave him a slight smile. ''This man here, Lonnie LaRue, is the arsonist. He was trying to frame Turner, just as Anthony said.''

''Why should I believe this Anthony?'' the sheriff asked. ''I don't even know who he is.''

''Because I'm telling the truth,'' Anthony said softly. ''At last I'm telling the truth.''

TURNER SAT WITH HIS BACK against a tree and Lacy in his arms. The sun had just risen over the horizon, and soon the layer of frost that blanketed the burned ground would be gone. The ugly blackened earth would once again be visible.

Sheriff Taylor had taken Anthony and Lonnie back to Claytonville. Lacy and Turner had promised to bring the horses down and get in touch with the sheriff as soon as they made the trip. As the sun climbed the eastern sky, Turner had everything in the world he wanted in his arms.

''It could have been so much worse,'' he said to Lacy.

''I know, but I can't help but think of all the little creatures.''

''Animals are smarter than you think. They have ways of escaping, and this was a small fire, very small compared to what it might have been.''

"I know," Lacy said. "But aside from the damage to the wilderness, you lost all your research."

Turner chuckled. "I hate to destroy the image of myself as a rugged man unfettered to the modern world, but I did have most of it backed up on a computer. I have an office at Pablo University in San Antonio. I'm going back there to teach next year."

He felt the surprise in Lacy as she sat up. "You're giving up the life of roaming the wilderness?"

"The search for the white panther was to be my last quest for a myth. I had hoped the legend might be true. But whether I ever saw the cat or not, I was determined to change my life. I guess I'd come to realize that, more than searching for myths, I was hiding from life."

Lacy nodded and gently lifted a hand to touch his cheek. "You deserve a life of happiness, Turner. You've had so much sadness."

"A lot of it was because I wouldn't fight for myself. If people wanted to think I was the kind of person who started fires, I wasn't going to dispute that. I made myself an easy victim for Lonnie LaRue." Turner was still astounded. "Who would have thought he started the fire that killed my brother? All of these years, I've wondered how that fire happened. My parents were so careful."

In a way learning the truth was like suffering the loss of Benjamin again.

"Lonnie's only a few years older than you. He must have been in college when his father lost his business. I gather it destroyed his family."

"But my father didn't intend to put anyone out of business," Turner said. "He was a good man. As president of the bank, he tried to help a lot of people.

Some, like the LaRues, simply couldn't dig out. The bank foreclosed on them.''

"But Lonnie was driven to retaliate, and the way he chose was to set your family's home on fire. What a horrible tragedy.''

"And then he kept tabs on me, popping back into my life. The irony is that it was the fire he set in Jackson Creek that sent me to St. Martinsville, and ultimately crashing back into his life. When that office burned, I moved on, as usual. That's when I heard a story about a strange creature in the swamp. I was at loose ends, so I made the move to St. Martinsville to pursue the legend. I guess in Lonnie's twisted mind, my father had taken his family, and then there I was, taking the woman he'd fallen in love with.''

"Life can certainly take some strange twists,'' Lacy said.

"Do you think he really loved Lilith, or did he just want her because I loved her?'' Turner asked. He knew it was a question that would always follow him.

"I don't think we'll ever know that.'' Lacy settled back into his arms. "I'm not certain even Lonnie knows.'' She brushed a kiss on his cheek, and Turner closed his eyes in pleasure. Lacy was the best thing that had come into his life in a long long time.

"What will happen to Anthony?'' she asked.

"He's in trouble for helping set those fires.'' Turner hated it in a way. Anthony had suffered enough. "He might have gotten over Lilith's death if Lonnie hadn't continued to feed him bitterness and anger. I think, deep down, Anthony's not a bad man.''

"I agree,'' Lacy said.

"Well, you got your story,'' Turner teased. "And a whole lot more than you bargained for.''

"I did indeed." She twisted to press warm kisses to his jaw and down his neck. "I got my story and I got my man."

"I can't believe you want to stick with me," Turner said.

"Heck, you're the best source I've ever met. I can just draw from your life to constantly create sensational tabloid stories. I mean, I can see the headlines now. Fire Starter Ignites Passions, or maybe, Too Hot to Handle."

Turner slipped his hands onto her ribs and gently tickled her. "I don't want to be the focus of your journalistic career. I want to be the focus of your love and passion and—"

He stopped when her lips made contact with his. Lacy was fun to spar with verbally, but she was a lot more fun to kiss, and touch, and love.

"We'd better start back to civilization," Lacy whispered in his ear. "The sheriff will be expecting us by the end of the day and my editor is waiting for a phone call."

"I didn't realize you were so eager for another horseback ride," Turner said. His hand slipped from her ribs to her breast. "I have an offer for you. Lots of fresh air involved." His fingers gently teased her skin. "But first, one question. The story of Aunt Belle and the White Panther—was it true?"

Lacy smiled. "Of course it's true. I don't make up stories. I tell the facts. And as to your offer, I think a ten-hour ride will supply plenty of fresh air. Make another offer."

He shifted her in his arms so that she had to look into his eyes. "How about a lifetime of love?"

He saw that his question surprised and also pleased

her. "A lifetime of love," she said slowly. "Does it come with any kind of guarantee?"

"Indeed. It's not a shoddy brand of love," Turner answered. "It's one hundred percent guaranteed, by a man who knows how important loyalty and honesty and courage are. This man also happens to have found a woman with all those qualities, and he isn't going to let her get away."

Lacy sighed. "I think this is going to make the best story ever written."

Turner laughed. She was completely one-track and incorrigible, and he loved her with all his heart.

"Just say yes," he whispered.

"Yes," Lacy said.

LACY LEANED FORWARD to accept Turner's kiss, which would seal their engagement. She had never dreamed that in accepting the assignment to write a story, she would change her life in the most profound way.

Just as her lips met Turner's, Buster gave a loud shrill whinny and began to scramble on the rocks. M&M, too, seemed spooked.

"What on earth?" Turner said. "After the fire, there shouldn't be an animal within ten miles of here." He sat up and helped Lacy to her feet. Together they walked to where the horses were still prancing and blowing.

"Easy, fellas," Turner said.

Lacy gathered M&M's reins and scanned the area. "Look!" She saw something moving in some underbrush that hadn't burned. "Look!" she cried again as she caught something white flash through the low scrub.

She felt Turner's hand on her arm, could sense the excitement running through him.

"Lacy," he said, pointing to the west, "it's the panther."

She saw it then, a magnificent cat. The panther came out of the underbrush and stood for a moment on a rock. It looked straight into her eyes. Lacy stared back, caught by the creature's presence. It was totally white, a magical animal. It stood, tail twitching in the bright morning sun.

"I almost don't believe this," Turner whispered.

Lacy didn't answer. She touched his arm. "She's leaving," she said, just as the cat turned and darted away. "She won't be back here."

Turner put his hands on Lacy's shoulders and turned her to face him. "Why do you say that?"

"She told me so," Lacy said, shrugging. "She was only waiting here for you. She wanted you to see her. She wanted you to always believe in the power of myth, and your ability for happiness."

Turner looked deep into Lacy's eyes. "*She* told you all that? And how do you know it was a she?"

Lacy stood on tiptoe and kissed him solidly. "Let's ride. I want a hot bath and a big bed."

"You didn't answer my question," Turner said.

"I guess you'll just have to read my story," Lacy said. "It'll be under the byline Lacy Wade McLeod."

In October 2001
Look for this
New York Times bestselling author

BARBARA DELINSKY

in

Bronze Mystique

The only men in Sasha's life lived between the covers
of her bestselling romances. She wrote about passionate,
loving heroes, but no such man existed...til Doug Donohue
rescued Sasha the night her motorcycle crashed.

AND award-winning Harlequin Intrigue author

GAYLE WILSON

in

Secrets in Silence

This fantastic 2-in-1 collection will be on sale October 2001.

HARLEQUIN®
Makes any time special ®

*H*ugh Blake,
soon to become stepfather to
the Maitland clan, has produced three
high-performing offspring of his own. But
at the rate they're going, they're never going to
make him a grandpa!

There's *Suzanne*, a work-obsessed CEO whose Christmas spirit
could use a little topping up....

And *Thomas*, a lawyer whose ability to hold on to the woman
he loves is evaporating by the minute....

And *Diane*, a teacher so dedicated to her teenage students she
hasn't noticed she's put her own life on hold.

But there's a Christmas wake-up call in store
for the Blake siblings. Love *and* Christmas miracles
are in store for all three!

Maitland Maternity Christmas

A collection from three of Harlequin's favorite authors

Muriel Jensen
Judy Christenberry
&Tina Leonard

Look for it in November 2001.

Two very different heroes. Two very different stories.
One gripping and passionate reading experience!

NIGHT AND DAY

A unique 2-in-1 from

HARLEQUIN®
INTRIGUE®

featuring editorially connected stories by:

ANNE STUART

and

GAYLE WILSON

Michael Blackheart and Duncan Cullen are as
different as NIGHT AND DAY. Yet they share a goal—
and neither man can imagine the dark world that
such a quest will take them on.

Available in November 2001 at your favorite retail outlet.

HARLEQUIN®

Makes any time special ®